GOVIND MISHRA

in the Glow of your Being

Translated from Hindi
by C.B. KARKI

THORNBIRD
NIYOGI
BOOKS

Published by
NIYOGI BOOKS
Block D, Building No. 77,
Okhla Industrial Area, Phase-I,
New Delhi-110 020, INDIA
Tel: 91-11-26816301, 26818960
Email: niyogibooks@gmail.com
Website: www.niyogibooksindia.com

Editor: Gita Rajan
Design layout: Nabanita Das

ISBN: 978-93-89136-33-3
Publication: 2020

Printed at: Niyogi Offset Pvt. Ltd., New Delhi, India

Machli, Machli, Kitna Pani[1]

(Hey fish, how deep are the waters)

She, in a black coat, was a few steps ahead of me. Below the overcoat of near ankle length, only a fringe of her sari just above her feet was visible. She was breezing along with the pace and grace of a deftly steered speeding boat that leaves behind a trail of furrows seething with eddying water.

The bare part of her neck between her hair and coat as also her swinging hands revealed her fair complexion. Her shoulder-length hair was braided in school-girl style twin pigtails, held in place with rubber bands.

On reaching the front of the building, she lifted her sari a little to climb the steps. Up the stairs, she walked briskly across the corridor towards her destination, her firm steps making a crunching sound on the coir carpet. Straight as an arrow, she whizzed her way into a corner hall. I stumbled behind her like a stone flung from afar, almost bereft of momentum. I, too, was headed for the same meeting.

---

1 The chapter title is based on a Hindi nursery rhyme and a game played by children. In the context of the chapter, it signifies the protagonist testing the waters before venturing deeper.

It was a circular air-conditioned hall, coloured curtains glimmering in the reflected light. People were converging from all directions for the meeting. Front-row chairs were meant for the VIPs; behind them, seats for their aides, and further behind for the rest of the participants. The principal actors of the conference continued to troop in. Those who had already arrived were engaged in animated conversation, obviously to show off.

The usual razzle-dazzle, hustle-bustle of a conference before it gets going. People hurrying, hopping around; no sooner had they got to their seats than they would leapfrog to be close to somebody else. The babble of voices reminded me of a lake in my town, rather a pond that remains dry in summer, at that time reduced to an ugly pit; as soon as it fills up with rainwater, it comes into its own. From out of nowhere, all sorts of creatures descend upon it. Frogs outnumber them all – leaping, jumping, landing here and there with a thud. And the pond resounds with their ceaseless croaking.

It was difficult to imagine a person like her in such an inelegant setup, but there she was … like a lighthouse throwing a throbbing beacon of light all around.

Getting up from her chair, as she went towards the table in the centre to pick up a copy of the agenda, I chanced to come face to face with her. I felt as if I was right in front of a luminous object. Inadvertently, I must have been on a collision course with her … that, pausing for a moment, she had to look up. Even then, perhaps, it was not me she was looking for but her way; and the very next moment, without raising her head but avoiding me as if skirting some obstacle, she made her way back to her seat. Now we were in our respective seats in separate corners, mine being some five yards away from hers, in a different row. The corner where she was appeared lighted up. I wished to continue looking at the source of that light, but was scared of the glare. Nonetheless, I kept stealing glances intermittently. Beauty in its fullness that the eye invariably slid towards it. Fair skin with a pinkish tinge, chiselled features, restless eyes of a doe, and the freshness of youth fanning them all. The cool breeze emanating from her wafted across to me. She had all that is associated with beauty and was well aware of the fact. A middle-aged man sitting beside her asked her something; she dismissed him with a shrug. She didn't even deign to look at him just as she had treated me when I came in the way of her vision. I thought she was proud.

Next time when I looked in that direction, she appeared to be a different person altogether. Raised eyebrows, eyes rotating ceaselessly like a lighthouse beacon, encompassing everything in its range. Her face, puckered with tautness a little while ago, now wore a melting look.

A ray of light from that beacon touched me too … faint, yet enough to obliterate scars and scratches and give the skin a soothing smoothness. A gentle gush of breeze billowing the curtains, the feeling of freshness and peace after a bath, a mild sun giving warmth to grass shrivelled in extreme cold, a fountain of fragrance in a hilly terrain, the heady scent arising from parched earth when it receives the first showers. Varied were the fantasies I was delving into and floating in! At that moment!

She was now gazing elsewhere, but her face still retained the same visage of tenderness. The tautness of her features had mellowed into softness, tinged with innocence – not the innocence of early youth but that which is thrown on the face by inner compassion, empathy. Hers was a beauty that does not blur the ambient aura, rather one that irradiates it with a new sheen.

A hilly river emerging from some uncharted cavern in an unimposing mountain cascades down into a plain, drenching some villages on the outskirts and then joins a big brimming river. A brief journey yet assuming myriad forms. Somewhere, a current gurgling through an opening in a dam, flowing fast and furious and hurtling down as a cataract at some others, elsewhere a placid lake, still and serene. Crystal-clear sweet water, white in summer and blue in winter. In summer oozing with affinity, in winter a little menacing. Somewhere too deep, even for an elephant, elsewhere just knee-deep, further down revealing every single grain of sand. However much you may pollute, it comes out clear the very next moment as it gurgles along on the pebbles. During winter and summer, what is just a narrow, steady stream swells into a raging torrent during rains, threatening human habitations. Water water everywhere, here yellowish, there reddish, elsewhere muddy. Floating garbage, grass, reed, and weed. Rotting thatches and door frames, parts of animal carcasses, occasionally a human body tossed around. As if bent upon a clean-up by washing away all sorts of filth and mud. Here and there, swirling currents of water, some just mild eddies while others awesome whirlpools in which once trapped there is no knowing where one is going to end up. The place where the river was just knee-deep disappears in the sprawling expanse of water.

Once the conference was over, the participants' patience lasted only till the VIPs' departure. Then all hell broke loose. Jostling participants, screeching chairs, rustle of papers, all contributing to the din. Someone was tilting the chair to get up, someone else was elbowing his way out through the crowd; some were talking animatedly, some were chewing betel or smoking, while some still remained seated. An onrush of people flooded the hall, just like flotsam and jetsam surge upwards when a still pond is suddenly disturbed.

While leaving, once again I crossed her path, this time deliberately. But she didn't even bother to raise her eyes. As if she was on a familiar terrain whose boulders and stones, dust and debris, and hurdles and obstacles were all known to her. Her gaze rooted to the ground, raising her sari a wee bit, she moved edgeways and walked away.

She can't disappear just like that!

A lovely face, like a rain-bearing cloud, emerged in the crowd out of nowhere, hovered over my head and heart, and in a jiffy I saw it vanish! It evaporated right before my eyes. I pinned my hopes on a chance meeting at some crossing or lane, in any public place or transport. Maybe I won't ever see her at all.

I can't simply let her vanish into thin air!

Someone was propelling me towards her, wherever she was. Relentless queries, untiring hunt, and following up all possible leads, ultimately I succeeded. The sixth storey of an office building, a series of coop-like cabins. One such was hers. She was sitting across the table.

She had wrapped a light green shawl around herself. Fair face, ruddy from the radiation of the heater. Amidst the chill of withering winter, an irradiant glow, the flame of life. Come, warm your hands against it.

'I am Anant' – further introduction after the name – director in such and such communication centre … sometimes writing too … Was it my real introduction or was I just recounting the compartments I was presently caged in? Office, rank, and the like … how far can they describe a person? They failed to arouse any interest in her. It was precisely this class she met day in and day out. No clue on her face to indicate that she had seen me only a few days back.

'Suvarna.' She didn't need to tell me that, as the nameplate was there outside – SHRIMATI SUVARNA CHOUDHARY.

'Coffee?' Her formal gesture found instant acceptance. How could I let go of a god-sent opportunity to prolong my stay?

Her face receding into the background, it was her eyes now all the way – those flickering eyes, myriad colours arising there, some iridescent, some light, others faint. Sometimes alternating, sometimes appearing together. There were tempests and tornadoes too, seemingly stalled at a point and tamed. In the seashells of her eyes lay the life force that could, in an instant, turn a surging flood into a gentle-flowing current.

Those eyes said a lot, held back a lot more. If only you could read the unsaid part, you would have laid your hands on the world's best literature.

'Kindly come to our centre to deliver a talk on the problem of communication....' I said, simulating the purpose of my visit.

'Me?'

Again those flickering eyes. Two birds flying in the sky ... everywhere. And yet nowhere.

'Yes, why not?'

'I mean what will I speak ... I can't even face an audience properly.'

The eyes opened their expanse for a moment. Their sheer beauty! A string cropped up ... holding one end of it, I began inching towards that vastness. Somewhere midway, out of modesty, she lowered her eyes, which changed to seashells again. I got stuck on her upturned nose ... an ideal you strive to rise to but never reach.

I beat a hasty retreat like a straw overwhelmed by the ocean's vastness. Seeing her again and from such close quarters, her face, which should have looked stale with familiarity, carried numerous hues yet new angles.

'You could give it a try. Delivering a speech is not at all difficult and that too in our country.'

I chuckled. She wasn't amused and looked at me rather coldly.

'You might feel a little nervous in the beginning. Then just remind yourself that the audiences are only a bunch of morons. Besides, I'll be close by.'

Not impressed, she wasn't looking at me … was looking nowhere, doubtful whether she was in the room at all.

'Do one thing. Put it down in black and white.'

The beautiful neck gave itself a jerk.

'Why? Do you really think I can't speak?'

'No, no! Our office insists on a written copy.'

Somewhat reassured, she was still undecided and began to look here and there; uneasy movements in the chair as if waves of crystalline water rippled in some narrow creek.

'Can't promise. Delivering a speech isn't my cup of tea. Never written one either. Let me think it over.'

'I'm sure you won't disappoint me.'

'What makes you think so?'

'A hunch.'

She looked quizzically at the man sitting before her. What sort of a person is he? Instead of proceeding step by step, he jumps to conclusions, then stays put there. Strange!

'I can't commit right now,' she said vaguely.

'No problem. I'll call and check up.'

Anant had guessed right. Next day Suvarna found herself ready to deliver the talk. Of course her reasons were different and personal. She should try to get over her inhibitions and qualms. Here was an opportunity to do something new, to explore hidden talents within oneself. Besides, these days one should be adept at delivering speeches. You never know when you are called upon to do so. It does give a boost to your personality. She gave her consent on the phone.

After the talk, we had tea in my room; just the two of us. I complimented her. She knew I would. So it didn't interest her much. But she had really spoken very well. Once or twice I had sort of interpolated, giving thrust to her viewpoint more with the intent of reassuring her. That had not gone down well with her, as was evident from the look on her face. Now, while hearing the praise, her face wore the same look. I thought I'd better revert to the content of the talk. 'The fundamental question is whether the meaning of a word is what a speaker or a writer gives it or that which is understood or absorbed by the listener or the reader.'

'I think it's somewhat both. That's how a message goes from one person to another.'

'If the message reaches anyhow, the question of the innate power of the word still remains. Where does a word derive its power – from the speaker or from the listener?'

'I will still maintain that it is both ways. Language is not unidimensional.'

'It isn't a question of language but of communication. And the problem of communication arises first at our own level. We have to first articulate our thoughts to ourselves and then think of communicating them.'

'I think it is complicating the issue,' she said. 'It's quite possible that the moment we think of communicating something to another, it begins to clarify itself to us. Actually, it's that stage where an idea becomes communicable. If conveying an idea to others is not the objective, then where is the need for communication at all? As simple as that!'

'Can we always claim that whatever we said we meant that way only and it was also understood precisely the same way?'

'The problem you are talking about might crop up in matters of gravitas, intellectual deliberations, or philosophical discourses. In our day-to-day interactions, however, we are able to say what we mean and it is also well understood.'

'Don't you agree that language distorts that which we want to convey?'

'Sometimes. But not always.'

'We resort to mediums other than language to express our most precious thoughts or feelings, don't we?'

I was looking into her eyes. She had seen through my naughty intent, for just then a flicker of exhilaration ran through those piercing eyes and a smile was about to spring. Promptly, she held it back.

'That may be so. But of all the means of communication devised by human, language is not only the most powerful but also the most scientific.'

Not only could she think logically, she could also articulate. She relished reasoning, the cut-and-thrust of discussion – an attribute commonly associated with men. She enjoyed getting to the root of a matter. She was curious to know and put to test what she knew. We chatted for quite a while.

'Let alone conveying to someone, I am often at a loss to fathom my own feelings.'

'You express yourself rather too well,' she laughed to sort of reassure me. That face inspired, as if it were the very corner you were frantically looking for to pour all of yourself, your entire being.

'My childhood was spent in a village and a small town where your thinking gets inhibited; feelings and beliefs too. Words don't come handy. If I try to be frank, it might as well be taken as unbecoming. English education opened me up a little. However, now I feel that while too much restraint and suppression might not be desirable, neither is stark openness, which often degenerates into nudity. Beauty, draped a little here and concealed a little there, is more fascinating. Likewise, emotions under control are more powerful than those gone berserk. I think I am a confused person.'

'Who … you?'

'Who else?'

'But you appear to be all right.'

'I don't know but exposure to English has made me appreciate our native things much better.'

'It's also possible that after your English education, you cling to things native all the more.'

'Even if it's so, what's wrong with it? By plumbing deeply and sensing what lies inside me, I'll get more strength than by transplanting it with something from outside. Maybe, in my case, this is how it should be, though what I feel about me presently is that I'm still open … of course drifting. And this has made me a lazy fellow. Thus far, whatever happened in my life happened in spite of me. Sent for education, got busy with it – starting from a village, to a school in a small town, and then to a city-like town. When an undergraduate, I saw the broad tarred road for the first time and was wonderstruck. I began wearing trousers only when I was studying for post-graduation. Thereafter, like other boys, I too was looking for a job. On getting a job, I'm now stuck in this groove. Had someone got me married, I would have fallen in that rut. That not happening, I am presently in the other one.'

'Parents?'

'Mother passed away long back, father when I was doing my MA. I've an uncle. In his lifetime, father had sold some landed property and deposited the proceeds in a city bank for my studies. Since joining service, I have been hopping from one city to another. And now this metropolis.'

'Why didn't you marry?'

'No particular reason. My uncle thought that being in a city, I would marry on my own, someone whom I liked. I didn't come across any. Those I met couldn't keep company even for a couple of years, let alone embarking on a voyage of a lifetime. Meanwhile, what I read and witnessed – its effects or, shall we say, ill-effects – led me to think that we could accomplish what we wanted to only by not marrying.'

'What do you wish to accomplish?'

'Don't know, but anything will be better than marrying.'

'You're making fun of us married people, aren't you?'

'No. What I mean is you come to raise a family after marriage. Bringing up children, getting them educated and settled – that becomes the primary goal. So many are already doing it. Whatever I wish to do should be something different; from that at least.'

'What's the certainty that you'll be able to accomplish that something? Any success so far?'

'Trying to find out … but had I married, even this quest would have slipped by.'

She was quiet; her gaze direct, staring deep into my eyes for the first time.

Those eyes, always on a flight like a bird with fluttering wings, could also be still and penetrate deep.

'I keep a diary about my voyage, trying to crystallize my thoughts. Frankly speaking, all this is just a facade. To put it simply, it so happened that I didn't get married and am now over age.'

'I see. You must be fifty now.' She was now flippant, teasing.

'Thirty. Half the life is gone. This is where you start feeling that the remaining half will fade away likewise.'

When and how did I come to reveal my innermost self to her, disregarding the fact that so far it was just an acquaintance? Of what interest could my personal trivia be to her?

But she listened patiently as a cultivated person would listen to a bumpkin's rants; instead of making fun she was condescending like a seasoned veteran. I kept on narrating other details of my uneventful life as well and with such eagerness that if I didn't do so, her eyes would unearth them anyway. Those eyes gave a soothing touch to my slurred speech and blurry statements … as if she knew my feelings better than I did and had already lapped them up.

Sitting before her, I wasn't dazzled by her beauty; rather felt affection emanating from her. Why does every beauty come with this undercurrent of love? May be the beholder's helplessness or yet another facet of beauty, or both. Beauty, thy name is sweetness of love!

'I feel a strange affinity towards you.'

'Really!'

Pleasure, surprise, and question, all rolled into a single exclamation. It came out with a smile, which carried it on till its echo lasted.

In the same breath, she got up. 'I'd better leave now.'

'What's the hurry?' I couldn't help pleading.

'No, no, must go. Work would have piled up by now back there in the office.'

27 December 1976

The swift pull of a kite's string!

High above, a tautly strung kite, stationary in the air, smiling to itself, much above the capers of kites flying below, suddenly nosedives for a dogfight with a kite below, drags it, and whizzes along in another direction. Whoopee! That other kite severed from its lifeline string! The predator kite not only cut it off from its moorings but also managed to entangle it in midair and flew along with it as the legit spoil of a victor.

Attributes quite different from mine, all aligned in a beauty are before me. I have never been intimate with any family of this class. Not that I have never before met or known persons with such attributes, but not like this, at one place, draped in such radiant beauty – as if rewards of those attributes converged in one being, thereby decorating themselves further.

It is not she who is trying to pull me, but it's me who is getting drawn towards her.

The way I was brought up and educated – in a village, then in a town – what did it give me? A mindset of indifference, lethargy, defeatism. Taking the peaks and troughs of life with stoicism, and in the process be a loser. Feeling of guilt in celebrating achievements, rejoicing only in losing. Shying away from venturing forward, more than content in lagging behind. Less trust in man, more in divinity; fatalism at every step. Self-confidence just a cipher, always wrapped in a pall of melancholy. Being tossed about like flotsam in a rough sea, ageing prematurely, to pass away unmourned.

And here is she – life force incarnate, bubbling with warmth, every fibre of her being aglow with self-confidence. Crystal clear as to what she wants and conscious of her ability to acquire it. A bundle of verve and vivacity, forging ahead relentlessly. Rejoicing in her existence and imparting a feeling of élan to others. Ever jolly, no trace of sadness for miles. Only that matters which is before you. Such brightness that spreads out like a ray piercing the veil of darkness, replacing it with light. No speculating or chasing mirages, simply living life as it unfolds.

She burns like a light … what iridescence, what divine fragrance!

Am I running away from myself? No, I am used to my loneliness. In fact, I've begun to derive pleasure out of this reclusive existence. I have my job, which keeps me occupied and fairly contented. I derive some feeling of sublimation through occasional writings. I've a few friends and also the company of books that prevent a feeling of vacuity within me. If there is escapism, it is my bachelorhood, my petty mundane existence. I'm aware that the outside is fraught with problems galore; so I am fairly smug in my small world, where I sit crouching. Nothing can easily pull me out of this cosy nest. But presently, what is before me appears to be different from what I am used to. It needs to be probed further.

Only curiosity? No, there is something more. What's it? Don't know.

A Pensive Princess

It was the first shower of that winter. A film of mist hung around, floating aimlessly in the buzz and whizz of the wind. All day long, a greyish darkness had hovered over the streets, a miasma of depression and dreariness. Dull haziness hung all over. Try to feel or fathom it, you would find neither water, nor cloud. Streets, trees, and buildings, all were enveloped in this freakish mood that nature chose to display today.

'How about visiting the exhibition? It's the last three days,' she asked after tea.

'Let's go.'

Chance to go out with her, in the very third meeting. Did she get this close with anyone so early as to go out with him in such a bleak weather, especially when it was going to be stark dark very soon?

'How long do you plan to be there?'

'As long as we want. Are you in any hurry?'

'No, not me, I was thinking about you. You have to reach home.'

'That I will. You think I would get lost in the exhibition?'

'I mean your husband will be waiting for you.'

'Oh!' she laughed. 'You're very caring. Please don't worry. He's not going to worry either. He is coming too, will be with us.'

We were to go separately. She with her husband, I by myself. I set out earlier. We were to meet at the exhibition gate, where she introduced me to her husband, Ramesh, a commonplace name matching a nondescript personality in good trim, innocent-looking. Disinterested in the exhibition, as in any other thing, maybe he was there only to humour his wife. With me, a formal handshake sans warmth. No deliberate disregard, just plain indifference. At first, while advancing to meet me, his eyes did betray some curiosity, which, however, vanished soon thereafter.

Suvarna was wearing a black pullover. As usual, her hair was tied in two plaits, but with red ribbons instead of rubber bands. The two small plaits lent their tautness to her frame, the red ribbons transmitting their lustre to her face. Whenever I found myself walking by her side, I longed to get closeted within the warmth of beauty and love. When we chanced to walk very close, an emotional wave would surge inside – sound of first musical notes heralding the *aalap*. Just then, she would outpace me.

She was darting hither and yon, with a spring in her step … her eyes a mixed bag of excitement and wonder. In her exuberance, she would abruptly leave us some paces behind. Somewhere she would make a sudden dash into the crowd with curiosity, like a child drawn to a spectacle.

Then that group of men would suddenly light up. People started staring at her. Initially unaware, the moment she felt she was being ogled at, she would withdraw in some embarrassment. To be beautiful is a crime in this country.

'Oho! Look here ... children's books ... let's buy some.'

She was pulling Ramesh. Her childlike act was in striking contrast to Ramesh's staid and sober demeanour of the elderly. He followed her mechanically to the book stall. They scanned through the books for a while. She would select books from this pile or that and bring them over to Ramesh to seek his nod. Ramesh would simply acquiesce. When the selected books had been duly collected, Ramesh quietly paid for them. This way they purchased some more books from other stalls.

Moving around, sometimes she was with me, sometimes with Ramesh, and sometimes all by herself. At those times, she was out of our sight. After a while, she was spotted looking for us in the crowd like a lost child. On locating either of us, she would come running. Sometimes she would get lost in the surging crowd and I would be looking for her. But Ramesh would not bother. He would calmly wait for her in a corner. After a round or two, she would reach him.

'What do you do on Sundays?' she asked while leaving. Ramesh as before – quiet, distant.

'Nothing particular.'

'Then come over some day to our place. We can spend time chatting.'

Chatting … with whom? On what topic? Chitchat. Only a pretext. Pretext for what …

'Ramesh will also be there … won't you, Ramesh?' she asked him, or just uttered those words looking at him. He gave a perfunctory nod. 'Give a ring before coming.'

I bade them goodbye. Saw them getting into the car, leaving, and me being left behind.

Suvarna's house … single-storeyed. Lawn in front, flower plants all around. Kitchen garden in the backyard. A swing in the veranda for the young and the old. A thick creeper, coiled around a side pillar, reaching out to the ceiling.

From outside, that small building nestling in the midst of trees seemed to radiate an aura of mystery, as if it were a castle of sorts. Foliage on three sides, one side the bright red sandy path I walked on to reach the doorstep. The absence of human movement made the sprawling lush greenery look barren. Reaching the veranda, I searched for the bell and pressed it. The ringtone resembled a bird call. Shuffling footsteps towards the entrance. A servant opened the door, led me in, beckoned me to a seat, and disappeared without a word.

It was a drawing-cum-dining hall. Sofas draped with coloured covers looked all the more colourful in the hazy light percolating through the window curtains. The décor on the walls was quite tasteful – some framed tapestry, some pictures, one or two abstract paintings. Specimens of creature comfort were also present – a heater to warm in winter, a cooler fixed in a window to take care of the summer, and a large fridge occupying a corner. Obviously the entire arrangement was by design. Every item in place, meticulousness in the choice of size and number of furnishings – neither excessive, nor deficient. A six-piece sofa-set, two low stools, four side tables. In one corner a record player. Alongside the dining table stood a glass cupboard with sparkling crockery; the rack near the record player was stacked with books, mostly English.

Proportion, balance, and taste visible everywhere, nothing haphazard or out of place. Top of the rack was decked with two framed photographs – she and Ramesh in one, two kids with cherubic smiles in the other.

The ambience of a typical urban dwelling, encircled by a bastion of upper middle-class security. Inside modern conveniences painstakingly collected; one could lead a carefree life just with them – making good those missing, adding a few now and then.

Celebrating festivals like Dussehra, Diwali, and other similar occasions with ritualistic formality in a stereotyped fashion must be the norm there. Holi must have been labelled crass and lumpen, not worthy of celebration in these pristine surroundings. Worship woven into daily chores like PT in a school. The days celebrated with zing and zest would be birthdays, New Year's eve, but in the course of a year such festivities would only be but few. Newspapers, of course, to sustain the illusion of being really educated. Some magazines, more for their illustrations than for their content; attending parties in the social circuit and some music records. The occasional cropping up of some office news like transfer of someone from one assignment to another, promotion, etc. could be the subject of an animated discussion on occasional evenings, only to be consigned to oblivion the following day.

It must have been decided beforehand where I was to sit. Perhaps the arrangement that was in place there had also taken into account how guests and visitors were to be looked after. They are welcome; some fresh air to be wafted inside, provided that …

Her voice inside … she was calling her servant and Ramesh.

She and Ramesh emerged and sat near me. We got talking. Starting with my rank, exchanging sundry information, some serious discussion thrown in between. My being single also cropped up somewhere. That too was merely commonplace information for Ramesh, though it shouldn't have been so as Ramesh had not learnt about my bachelor status in our first meeting. Marital status is taken for granted for a man of my age, so information of my bachelorhood seldom fails to evoke a ripple of surprise for a new acquaintance.

Ramesh started getting bored as soon as the talks veered away from service matters. This always happens … she knows. Ramesh is made that way – will give company so long as the talks relate to tangible matters. The moment they deviate, he begins to lag behind. Talks, on their part, also tend to gradually get rarefied – head towards the abstract – that's the only way to understand the core of things.

Ramesh got up … talking, talking all the way! Empty talks. What pleasure do you get out of it! What's so rare, so unique in a rank outsider that you get immersed in a tête-à-tête with him? One can appreciate social visits and inter-family goodwill visits, but to get tied around such tittle-tattle … to lose yourself in it? No harm in some visitors coming, but dragging on like this? Isn't his family self-sufficient? Household chores, stress, and tension of office … these are the real stuff. And enough too. How can you spare time for such talks? It seems that idle airy-fairy talking is also an opiate, an addiction.

Thus, only the two of us kept up the conversation. Suvarna was a cerebral woman. At times she almost sounded like an intellectual. Interest in all sorts of things and a fairly good understanding of them … also the curiosity to delve deeper. Actually, it was her conversation that didn't match the atmosphere or décor of the house, else even her perfectly proportioned features would have looked nothing more than a part of household furnishings. But for the standard of her conversation, she might just have looked a typical housewife.

'You've kept the house very well.'

'To be a housewife is a matter of pride for me,' she said with a smile. 'I enjoy my domestic chores as I do my office work. Just as I want to succeed in my official duties, I want to be accomplished in my home. There I don't want to lag behind any man, here behind any woman. I do my best … looking after the children, managing the house, attending to Ramesh …'

She actually does care for him. Knowing Ramesh's nature, she wants to bring him to the fore everywhere, so that he doesn't feel neglected. She pushes Ramesh forward before any new acquaintance from the very beginning. But in no time he retreats into his shell. Surprising that he does not realize that getting to know a new person is akin to exploring a new country. She can't help it if she happens to impress people more than Ramesh is able to do. Inadvertently then, she comes to dominate, making herself special and Ramesh secondary. This is felt even by those who were originally associated with Ramesh only. She hopes that Ramesh will eventually come round. Entrenched habits take time to change. At least, all this has led Ramesh to accept that his wife has her own individuality and can have her own circle of acquaintances and friends. Ramesh should also know about her circle, so she always carries him along, despite his reluctance.

'It's wrong to say that a woman can't perform as efficiently as a man,' she was saying. 'Today's woman is disproving it.'

'There is no denying it. At the same time, gender rivalry is uncalled for. Why should a feeling of comparison agitate women's minds at all?'

'Man starts it. Unnecessarily, he credits himself as being more adept in coping with the existential struggle.'

'A few may think so. I believe that the spheres of duty of the two are separate.'

'No, it isn't so. They can be one and the same.'

'Home?'

'Now this for example. It is man's decision – arbitrary, if I may say so – that home is woman's domain. Why shouldn't it be man's too? They should share household work, fifty-fifty.'

'Could it be achieved here, in your home?'

'Almost … I've drawn Ramesh in domestic affairs. He doesn't do much; it is because I'm rather too involved. This is my home. So I want to personally attend to the minutest of details. I'm rather overly careful not to let my home suffer owing to my official duties.'

'Such a deep interest in home is probably in your genes. Besides, home is always a woman's first love.'

'This is my nature, I admit, but positively not because I'm a woman. Many women do not relish being homebodies. That attitude also deserves respect, whereas they're dubbed as odd characters. In my opinion, every woman should take up some work outside home. Thus only will she fulfil herself. I wasn't in need of money, but after marriage I took up the job.'

'In the West, high incidence of broken homes after the Second World War is attributed to more and more women going out to work.'

'What is a home? Certainly it's not bigger than life that the latter be crushed under it. It is a home only when both strive equally to make it so, else it's already broken. We Indians, in particular, often continue to accept a grave as home. The westerners are more honest. A home is either a home or it is not … as simple as that. Oh silly! I'm inflicting a lecture on you … '

She laughed … either she was laughing at herself or was simply pleased with self. Meanwhile, the servant brought tea and she got busy in making tea.

'Sorry, talked a lot. Now you tell me – what are your interests?'

'Reading … lots of reading.'

'How nice! I, too, am very fond of reading. What do you read?'

'Mostly novels … literature, history, sociology also. No specific choice or genre, whatever takes my fancy or comes my way. Why do you read?'

'I relish it, can't go to sleep till I've turned a few pages of a book. What about you?'

'I read to unravel the meaning of life … taking cues from the thoughts of great people gone by. How little do we understand life!'

All of a sudden, Suvarna froze into silence. This man sitting in front … an ordinary sort yet special. Even the very first impression had been that he was guided more by the heart than by the head, which is why he seemed to have a certain aura of freshness about him. The first impression was now shaping into an enigma … life … understanding it … what's that!

She was looking silently at me, not even at me, was looking beyond me.... Her abrupt silence after non-stop chattering ... as if a kite sailing merrily in the air suddenly got entangled in the branch of a tree and was fluttering there.

The thoughtful face was now tinged with sadness. That elegant and spruced-up world of which she was the undisputed queen ... she should be playing with gems and pearls; or that favourite game of girls – tossing up pebbles and catching them; or should be getting ornaments made, disposing them or getting them remodelled to suit current fashions; or should be stitching up rag dolls and ripping down the dolls to design new ones!

In his world with a modicum of most creature comforts, Ramesh appears to be quite at home with a monotonous life, but Suvarna...? Sadness enveloping her face then indicated that she hadn't yet reached that stage of being rubbed out, where a person even ceases to feel the monotony ...

'I must take your leave,' I said, after finishing tea.

'Do come again. You live nearby?'

It was the third time that she had drawn me ... from office to exhibition, from exhibition to home, and now from home to home. In the beginning, how helpless I had felt before an expanse of beauty ... went floating far in it ... as if there was beauty ... just beauty. Now there was more to her than met the eyes – depths ... unknown, unseen, unfathomable. If only they could be plumbed!

If we could not give each other anything more than contrived chit-chat and formal reciprocal visits, it mattered little whether we met or not. There is plenty of that trash around both of us. For something beyond, we will have to slough off our cloaks – she her office and home, I my office and bachelorhood; she her metropolitan snobbery, I my townie complex. We do not even retain our individuality as unadulterated individuals, cursed as we are, to live in this mould or that.

She called Ramesh from inside. Both of them came out to see me off. A fixed routine like hanging a picture on the drawing-room wall facing the window.

Eyes, behind the hands folded in namaste. Eyes restive … trying to reach out to the distant twinkling stars. A young girl going missing in the exhibition and then rejoining her people or a princess lost in a forest …

Which one of these is she?

Tracks and Trails

'Hello-o-o-o-o.'

Stretching the o-o-o on the phone, the tone enquiring but dulcet, a tad songlike.

'What are you doing?'

'Why?'

'So sorry, the other day you had to wait unnecessarily and couldn't meet me.'

Last time I had occasion to go towards her office, and walked casually into her room as well. There was no one. Even then, I sat for a while and came away after dropping a slip in a table-drawer to say that I had come.

'Yes I'd thought of.... When can we meet?'

'Whenever you wish.'

'How about today, right now?'

Silence prevailed for a few moments at her end; then came her soft quivering voice, sounding like the movement of rain-bearing clouds. 'Where?'

'Why don't you come over here to my office?'

Had no intention of asking her to come that far and trouble her ... but it just happened. And she readily agreed, sort of making amends for my futile wait for her that day, even though she was not to blame for it.

Red sari with black polka dots, red blouse. The red accentuated the glow on her face. Eyes drooping while smiling. Ruffled hair flying in the breeze.

'A glass of water, please,' she said the moment she entered, breathing heavily. 'Coming here took away so much time … then these people … how they stare … ugh!'

The door shut behind her automatically. I placed a glass of water before her. She had a sip or two and, then, absent-mindedly, started twirling the glass on the table.

I was overcome with a feeling of guilt. My office, a crowded place, I could have gone over to hers. But shrugging off the oglers' behaviour, she had come out of it soon – she had come to meet me after all, so why should she be distracted long by them – and here I was still stuck with those lumpens?

'This vulgar staring by these people, no doubt underlying is repressed sex,' I said. 'Indians alone stare like that. But I think, more than anything else, it is because of the baggage of boredom that we all carry with us in whatever measure.'

'There is boredom outside India. In Europe too. Probably, much more.'

'But people there do not look for its cure in sex. They are fed up with it; here it is still an alluring proposition.'

'No … no! This is sheer perversity, nothing else. If there is boredom, there are several ways to cope with it, not by harassing someone this way.'

'But why this boredom, have you ever given it a thought?'

'Any long-drawn humdrum existence will eventually land us into boredom, but you can't do without such an arrangement either.'

'You mean it is like the bullock going round and round in the oil press of yesteryears, getting used to it eventually.'

'That is seeing only the darker side of things. There is something positive too, such as the pleasure of a project completed to satisfaction in office, the pleasure of give-and-take in a family.'

'Then why does a thirst linger on?'

She lifted the half-filled glass to her mouth, her large eyes directed towards me. Did she have an answer ... restlessness certainly is there ... to see or feel something ... to accomplish, to be ... what? For a while she sat there as before, and then got up and moved to the window.

There was a breeze outside – midway between summer and winter, neither so strong as to blow things away, nor so mild that it could not be felt. Falling leaves went swinging in the air, landing some distance away from the tree to which they belonged. From there also, they were bound to be carried away further – God knows where. Simultaneously, inside her too, there was a whiff of commotion – goodness knows what, why ... the heart pounding in anticipation of some imminent changes.

As if the outside breeze was clawing its way inside ... each scratch with a prickle of heightened emotions.

'Are you happy with your life?' I asked her while making coffee.

'What do you think?'

'I think you are.'

'Then so it must be,' she said briefly.

'No, I meant … '

'See, it's very difficult. It all depends on how you interpret happiness. I've a fairly good job, family life is ok, parents and in-laws are all very nice….'

'You are lucky.'

'Well….' she laughed. 'But pray what way are you unlucky … let me hear that!'

'No, nothing like that … no misfortune of any sort. Had it been so, there would've been no time to brood over it. Maybe it is our destiny to remain imperfect under all circumstances. Either a person will be worrying about his livelihood or, if moneyed, will be suffering from this illness or that. If they happened to be like us, the questioning type, then they will be hovering around incomprehensible questions with a restless heart … no way will humans be happy. They say: be content. What it boils down to is, think that everything is hunky-dory and nothing needs to be done.'

'Even so, what's wrong about it?'

'Nothing. In another context, Ramkrishna Paramhans had asked us not to worry about the world because we have not made it. You say that one should not think about the self as well.'

'You're given to too much thinking. Right now enjoy your coffee.'

Saying this, she laughed … the echo travelling quite some distance, we two reverberating at two ends of it, both of us light and floating. Our surroundings had become very clean and bright, as if there was nothing but that silvery laughter and the two of us were immersed in it, were a part of it.

Sometimes Anant probes deep unnecessarily; is too inquisitive. He would ask questions like why I came here at all. Well, if I had replied that I came because I felt like it, should it not suffice? Actually such a question needn't arise at all. But Anant will so prick that Suvarna will brace up … why not trace the little thorn in the finger with a fine needle?

After coming out of the spell of her laughter, I got intrigued by another thing. Reaching a point, in the flow of a discourse, she so easily blunts the current that the arguments get diffused instantly … as if they were of no more significance than soap bubbles fizzling out in midair.

'Probably you believe only in what's before you.'

'Believe or not, our course of action is determined by reality alone.'

'What about our beliefs then?'

'When you have to act in pursuance of the reality before us, it's better to have suitable beliefs, else we'll turn out to be hypocrites in our own eyes.'

'How about having no beliefs whatsoever?'

'Nothing wrong with that either.'

I felt jolted. How is this possible? Willy-nilly, some beliefs do take shape … our priorities, our values … right or wrong.

She pretends as though she doesn't give much importance to thinking, while her views point to the contrary.

'Ok, tell me, what are we doing at this moment?'

'Having coffee.'

'Only that?'

'We are also conversing.'

'And…?'

'And what…?'

'Besides, we are thinking too … beyond our chit-chat we are thinking, may be something altogether different. Look how many layers exist – coffee, talk, followed by discussion, then thinking; one thought leading to another, sometimes something totally unconnected. Amidst all these activities, you appear to give top spot to coffee, something that at best deserves the last place.'

She didn't continue the discussion. Picking up a magazine lying on the table, she began to turn its pages idly. I felt a little upset. She came from such a distance and unnecessarily I embroiled her in serious discussion. Perhaps, the itch to make an impression had led me to go into overdrive! Normally, I never talk in this manner.

'Bored you?'

'Oh … ' she was startled. 'Not at all….'

'You feel fed up with such talk. In fact, sooner or later, we all find it meaningless.'

'No … the importance of discussion cannot be denied. It's through talks alone that we can share in each other's lives.'

'Not through talks alone … we do better through other methods; talks often remain superficial….'

'What magazines do you subscribe to here?'

We changed course. Names of magazines, office duties, books at home … kind of mundane information exchanged, followed by comments on each.

Even while conversing thus, the stream of exhilaration, which had sprung out on her arrival, continuously ran inside me. I realized that while enumerating various layers of existence during conversing, I had forgotten to include the most important one. Coffee, talks, thinking behind talks, thinking unconnected with the talks, vague something … but we were beyond all this mishmash. Something was brewing inside us just then and that alone was important.

'Got to go now … already quite late,' she said, reining her thoughts.

Her voice belied her words. And further contradicting her voice, she got up … contradiction after contradiction!

'So soon?'

'Dear me! One full hour has gone by?'

'Only *one* hour….'

'Is that nothing, dear sir?'

'An hour passed … so soon, didn't realize.'

'Neither did I.'

She rose from her seat and picked up her purse, but kept standing where she was. I went over to her … would accompany her downstairs to see her off. When I stood for the first time so close to her, I felt my being dissolving into hers. Whatever constituted my individuality was dripping down like blobs of molten wax. Now it wasn't me but a bouquet of air in my place. My head had slipped on to her neck.

Depth! That fair depth between her neck and shoulder … steady … steadying … taking care of me. There, multitudes of elements assembled to be me … a foetus awakening to life in a womb!

Living and dying together, so quick.…When I regained consciousness, there was nothing but fragrance. She was standing still even now, while in the meantime, I got immersed in God knows how many things. Something might have happened to her also, who knows. When I raised my head, my eyes were moist with silent gratitude. She before me, detached, unaffected, like an ascetic.

She paused only for a moment, then stepped forward and opened the door for herself. As she strode on, I followed her … the sound of our footsteps in sync amid the noise outside.

I opened the door of her car … she sat inside and shut it.

'So nice that you came.'

Her eyes closed once with a faint smile. Face like a pink lotus, swaying in the eddies of water … the moment when beauty transcends itself.

She was looking at me. Me descending into her eyes, just as a boat slips into the lake … slowly, noiselessly.

Somebody is knocking.

People want to see her. If she stops somewhere, they want to walk along with her. Walk together some distance, then they want to say something to her. If she listens, they start knocking … bang … bang … bang … bang.

In the office she meets everybody; even converses informally with some. She doesn't want to nurture any such complex that mandates dos and don'ts for a woman. When she was given a job, it was not contemplated that she would remain sitting still like a decked-up doll. If men can talk frankly without inhibitions, why can't she? If some people misunderstand, let them. Problem arises when people start knocking.

She has had everything easy since childhood. Only daughter after two sons … plenty of parental and familial love. A big mansion in the city, an army of domestics – car to ferry her to and from school.

'Jingle bells, jingle bells, jingle all the way,

Oh what fun it is to ride in a one-horse open sleigh.'

The slightest hint of tears in her eyes would fetch a mild reprimand from her parents, 'Don't be sentimental, my dear, reason it out.' Even before becoming a science student, she had learnt to apply her mind and logic. A man can achieve whatever he desires. His greatest strength is his intelligence with which he can turn his weaknesses into strength and advantage. Crying is foolishness; one can always remain happy by dint of intelligence. As for advancement … only intelligence can achieve it.

When she joined college, it was the same story. The cynosure of all eyes. Every boy eager to court her. Her slightest whim and the guy would feel obliged to indulge it. Meanwhile, she had also learnt the art of escaping; beauty teaches you! English novels like *Rebecca* and *Gone With the Wind* further honed her skill in wriggling out. How girls can quadruple the power of their beauty with the aid of intelligence – flirting yet keeping head above water, else you are in deep trouble!

Ramesh was in the same college. A simple, shy boy, aloof, keeping to himself. She had hardly ever looked at Ramesh properly. Five years later, all of a sudden, a marriage proposal popped up from Ramesh's family. When her parents asked, she gave her consent. No inadequacy was found on Ramesh's side – family quite respectable, Ramesh educated and of good character. Meanwhile, he had also secured a fairly good job. In-laws' financial position fairly sound, landed property too. There was no ostensible or valid reason to reject such a proposal. There was nothing to suggest that she had anyone particular in mind. So it just happened, as so many things just happen with her. She got married.

Somebody is knocking again.

Anant … restless eyes – deep and sad – in some quest, each moment breaking up under the strain of some dilemma … all of a sudden fell on her shoulder like a flower from a bough, falling plop on to your lap. The sensation of some living thing landing on the shoulder was tingling.

Confusion … as if it wasn't someone else's head resting there but an integral part of her own being, landing there to fill some void within. The sadness in Anant's eyes often looks like a reflection of her own gloom, much as she spurns misery, wants to be ever happy.

Nail-polished fingers on the telephone.

'How are you?'

'Good! And you?'

'What are you doing?'

'Just … '

'Come over … I'm here only.'

Beige-coloured silk sari and blouse. Dense hair … dry, fluttering even in mild breeze. Seeing me, her lips spread in a slight smile. Light lipstick.

'Why the sudden summons, Madam?'

'Just felt like it.'

Raging storms in the eyes. A singular turbulence emanating from there was spilling on to her face and then moving over the body, gentle ripples arising there, like the fluttering rough hair.

Fingers stirring a spoon in the teacup … slender fingers, nails further lengthening them, a ring on one finger of each hand. One ring studded with a pearl, the other with a diamond … the pearl round, the diamond oval-shaped.

On the pretext of seeing the pearl closely, I took her palm in my hands … touching the petals of a lotus. A thrill coursed through me. Quickly, she pulled away her hand.

'I like pearls more than diamonds,' she said.

'They suit you more.'

'Don't know.'

Was it mere coincidence that I happened to hold her pearl-wearing hand only – pearls that were her first choice?

'You wear quite a lot of gold.'

'Yes, I do, nothing unusual.'

'But girls educated in English-medium schools are not attracted to jewellery.'

'Why should I run true to type? Why should I necessarily like or dislike whatever others do or don't?'

My experience was different. One day a group of girls, ten to twelve years old, were walking by. Their mode of dress and style of speech, their language, tone, and tenor were almost the same … so much so that it was difficult to make out who was speaking. It appeared strange to me, the extent to which this education shapes everyone in the same mould, churning out in the process clones instead of individuals. Was not the be-all and end-all of education, its very purpose, aimed at nurturing and boosting individuality rather than inhibiting it? Similar demeanour, 'hi' on meeting somebody, 'bye' on departing. All men uncles, all women aunties. The same 'hi' between lovers and also between married couples.

Suvarna was rotating the gold bangles on her wrist. While rotating, her fingers would hold up the one studded with pearls. Even while playing with gold and pearls, she was actually detached from them. She had invited me, but appeared to have lost interest once I came. Previously, I had never seen her like this ... sort of lost, fumbling. If I asked something, at times she just kept quiet; she might have as well forgotten my question itself, sinking lower and lower in the chair ... as if wanting to yawn but unable to do so.

'Can't we meet outside some evening?' I asked her.

'When?'

'Any day.'

'Check up then.'

'You'll refuse?'

'Maybe. Find out then,' she repeated.

'Yesterday I was wondering why I can't meet your glance.'

'Why? Am I so terrible or horrible?'

'No, no. I mean look straight into your eyes.'

'No big deal. Go ahead, look at me the way you want to. In case you feel the glare, put on a pair of sunglasses. I do.'

'Do you also feel the glare?'

'The sun's glare, certainly.'

'Another thing. With a person of my age, I become informal in the very second meeting, but with you ... I feel scared.'

'But ... why?'

'Don't know.'

'Well ... yes, at times I can be nasty too, but you needn't fear.'

'If someday I become informal with you?'

'Give it a try.'

'No, not deliberately ... sometimes informality very naturally creeps in ... then.'

'Maintaining a little formality is also good.'

But something was amiss today. She wasn't bubbly and vibrant as on previous occasions. Some heaviness lay about her, like she hadn't slept well the previous night. Somewhere something had fallen apart … was in disarray … like surging floodwaters making a helter-skelter dash to breach the dam and every time being thrown back and ending as whirlpools.

'I'd better take leave now.'

Bit uneasy, first she quivered … while sitting … the quivering of a boat parked in the bank when it is untied and gets into the waters. The reddish tinge of roses appeared in the eyes.

She didn't say anything. Just kept looking at me going towards the door. Before reaching there, I turned around to have a parting glimpse only to be drawn back to her again.

One of her arms lay stretched on the table, fair and fleshy; she was clenching and unclenching her fist. My hand landed on it.

'Don't feel like going.'

Her closed fist opened, my palm slipped into it. Two fluttering leaves, fluttering all the more with mutual touch. Two beings floating in the cup of two palms.

Releasing my fingers slowly, she pulled the last finger towards herself and then let it go.

We should meet somewhere outside. This was a long-pending request of mine. Whenever we met, I would bring it up this way or that. I longed so much to be with her outside the office atmosphere. One day, when it really looked like a burning desire, she consented. As we were pondering over the place to go, all of a sudden, she said excitedly, 'Come on, let's go to the zoo.'

The days were getting longer. A week or so more, and winter would be far behind. Restlessness among birds and beasts was quite visible. No sooner had we entered the zoo than Suvarna put on her sunglasses, taking them off whenever she needed to see something clearly.

'A small train had been introduced here. Taking a round of the zoo in the train was a big draw for the visitors. Crowds multiplied, but the number of birds began to decline. The rattle of the train would scare them. So it had to be discontinued.'

Suvarna was a little surprised. 'The fort wall makes a good backdrop here,' she said.

We were talking while walking.

'Look up there … a man is peeping from an embrasure in the ramparts.'

'Where … oh … there? No, that's just a piece of cloth,' she insisted.

She stopped and stared for a few moments in that direction. After a while, that cloth-like thing moved.

'Yes, it's a man indeed. He was standing so still that he looked like a piece of cloth.'

'Several rooms have been built against the fort wall, and a number of people live there.'

'Really? Good that old structures are utilized thus. Finding accommodation is such a problem in this city. Come, let's go that way.'

We headed towards another direction. Suvarna was in high spirits, observing everything closely and commenting on it. I was watching her more than the things around me. It was springtime and Suvarna's cheeks were glowing in the mild warmth. To avert the sun, she would cover her head with a corner of her sari; pretty face in that frame looked still prettier.

Just ahead was an ice-cream vendor.

'Come, we will have an ice cream … orange bar.'

How easily she transforms into a little girl whenever she so desires, or, perhaps intrinsically she is a child. Licking the orange bar, we moved forward, lips and tongues getting redder. It was long back that I had had an orange bar, though in childhood it was the only thing we knew by way of ice cream.

'Come, let's run,' soon she put forth her second proposal.

While licking the ice-cream lollies, we began to run.

We slowed down or walked whenever short of breath. Thus, we walked a lot. She would suggest we hit the less-traversed trail whenever we came across one. On seeing a climb, she would tackle it running. A path leading to a cage was rough. She moved towards it. Ahead, on a raised ground, was an enclosure for birds built with wire netting as a roof and the pegs for the wire net fixed on the slopes … below lay a pit-like small field hidden from the net.

She stopped near the pegs watching the net. I was right behind her, almost touching her, my nostrils drenched with the heady fragrance of beauty. The whole ambience had livened up.

The enclosure was empty, grass growing here and there in patches. At last, in a shaded corner, we sighted a lonesome peacock.

'I suppose the enclosure is meant for beautiful birds,' I said from behind.

'Why do they put up the netting?'

'So that they do not run away.'

'Then why don't they have a netting in place for all the birds?'

'Small birds will fly away anyhow.'

'Why, a net can also be designed for them. But see, there are quite a number of small birds in the zoo and they are not captive – means they can be kept by adopting other means.'

'Beautiful birds are precious. They have to be guarded.'

She looked beyond; didn't somehow like the idea of birds in captivity.

'Somewhere around here are a number of colourful birds. In England, near Cardiff, I had seen a number of ducks, having red, yellow, blue beaks. Similar birds have been kept here too,' I said excitedly.

'Wow? Come, let's see them,' turning around, she narrowly escaped bumping against me. In our quest for colours, as we headed towards another direction, we passed by the area for monkeys. She had an aversion to them.

'They gawk awkwardly and howl irritatingly,' was her terse comment.

'They are our ancestors, aren't they?'

'That's why men also....How elegant a tiger is.'

'Elegant or cunning? The way it pounces on its prey!'

'It's purely instinctive. Its hunting style and skill. In all other respects, *it is* elegant. Come, I'll show you.'

Varieties of ducks and waterbirds swimming in the pond ... displaying multiple colours, some pure white, some pied ones, some lolling near the water's edge, some perched on trees, flapping their wings.

Now she was cheerful. The glum look a little while ago had vanished.

'What a riot of colours! All so lovely! But none as perfect as the white,' I said, after watching the birds.

'Sorry, I don't agree. See that yellow one, the red, and even the black. Each has its own charm.'

'They look fake. White surpasses them all, as it can absorb every colour; it invokes feelings of purity and simplicity, somewhat like that unalloyed beauty a person radiates unselfconsciously when one stands uncovered by any artificiality.' Looking at her, I felt I had complicated matters a little too much.

'What's artificial about other colours? All are natural in their own way,' she said.

'White is simple.'

'Simple? But that is no colour at all. The very meaning of colour is that which isn't simple.'

'But we can't do without the simple.'

'Colour is necessary. Just think how dull and drab the world would look without colours. I never feel sated with colours. As for nature … in any surrounding, you may chance upon a colour never seen before. So countless are the colours nature is teeming with that one life won't suffice to identify them all.'

Previously too, her intelligence had struck me, but this was the first occasion that I sensed how much her intellect was integral to her beauty … a fascinating combo of beauty and brains!

From there, we moved towards the habitat of tigers.

'See, how gracefully it walks. If there's such a thing as elegance, this is it. How exquisite the black stripes look on its skin,' she was pointing out to me. I agreed.

Sprawled before us lay nature, further beautified here and there by human hands. We had been walking for quite some time now. She was getting tired.

'You should routinely walk much more,' I was surprised at the intimate tone and content of my advice.

'I've been walking and walking. How much more do you want me to walk?' she whined like a kid. I had an urge to lift her in my arms.

We sat down on a cement bench. She had not an iota of worry that her silk sari would get dirty. She told me that some time back, she used to dance and was proficient, having learnt dancing professionally. She had had performances and dance recitals in several cities.

She gave it up because of the pressures of her job and household duties, mainly the children. She planned to take it up again. As we were talking, we noticed countless insects crawling up her sari.

'See, they are also hungrily seeking your company,' I joked.

'So should I take them along?' she muttered like a petulant child and got up to brush them off her sari. I, too, lent a helping hand.

'Let's go. They won't let us sit in peace.'

The grassy ground stretched ahead. Here and there under the cover of trees could be spotted romancing couples, lost in themselves, in their seemingly small but actually vast world.

'How life's beautiful moments come by themselves. One doesn't have to exert to bring them,' I said.

'Even if one had to exert, so what? They ought to be brought.'

'Does Ramesh know that you are strolling here with me?'

'Yes, I'd told him.'

'He didn't object?'

'What's there to object? It's me who will form my circle of friends, not Ramesh, just as I can't choose friends for him. Ramesh knows that I socialize with you. I've also told him that I like you.'

'You told him all this?' I was taken aback.

'So what? Did I say something wrong?'

'No. What was his reaction?'

'None whatsoever. He knows this is how I am; it's my nature. He understands me.'

While returning, we opted to walk amidst the foliage instead of taking the gravel path. Trees swaying in the breeze, rustling leaves, soft earth a little damp, our feet sinking into it. A building was half covered with a trailing creeper. On one side, there were short bushes passing over which the creeper had made its way upwards. Between the building and the bushes, there was a path, narrow but shaded and cool. Passing through it, we suddenly stopped … very close to each other, her head almost touching my shoulder, the fragrance of her hair wafting into my nostrils and then descending into my whole being. What an exquisite feeling within … exhilarating … blissful … grand, and every fibre of my body aglow with sheer delight.

Just a faint touch, but its ripple effect spreading far and wide. A mere moment, but how infinite! As if in that moment, someone has poured inexhaustible strength within me … now I was strong enough to keep going and endure any hardship that came my way. Life was beautiful despite all the lows.

3 March 1977

Life's journey … is it simply traversing the same road from dawn to dusk or are there byways and heights and depths too? If these exist, then why do we knowingly or unknowingly keep the major part of our lives filled with those things that just turn us over and over from morning to afternoon, from afternoon to ...

Is life only what's visible and tangible in front or are there also horizons beyond? Isn't it so for the simple reason that they are invisible, and the sole proof of their existence lies in our sensitivity? In that moment of closeness, I had a glimpse of those horizons. I want to touch them, but it might not be possible to do so just by trudging along the road. They are those horizons that cannot be reached by plodding on, but by rising up to them. It's said that individuality is a person's best possession. But if somebody's closeness boosts my individuality to such an extent that I begin to see beyond ... what of that? And if I have to reach out to those horizons only through intimacy with this person, then should I not hold his or her hand to attain this?

What are these horizons and what's their identity? Just as in the Himalayas, enveloped in mist, one peak is glimpsed here, another there, these horizons may be sighted, if at all, by someone, but only during special moments. We need to be blind to see them. With open eyes, we can only see one step forward and another backward. Often we remain in an arena of conflicting emotions – want to keep wide awake with eyes fully open and also seek the pleasures of closed eyes; want to cling on to life before us and also pine for the hidden. We want to acquire, but are mortally afraid of losing, and owing to this, maybe, we go on losing things that really matter, then console ourselves that the things lost were not worth acquiring.

Ever since I've met her, I've begun to feel and reflect more. Myriad questions arise in my mind! A host of beautiful and yet more beautiful ideas are blossoming, as if someone has come and fired me with the zest of living! I feel I'm not alienated from things outside me but am in sync with them, and they are there to bestow perfection upon me … I'm an integral part of it all. If you're obsessed with one person, your world should shrink; contrarily, my world is expanding exponentially. I want to bond with everything, every being.

Once I felt that if you wish to unravel the purpose of life, look at children. How the flame of life lights up their eyes. Curious to know everything, keen to take in everything. Closeted in love. Returning doubly the love they get. Mischief too, but harmless and innocent. How they live huddled close to life, seeking warmth from it and generating warmth in it.

Am I being born?

Lotus Roots

A grove of tall trees, entangled branches overhead, the ground at their feet opening up in stray by-lanes. As the twilight hour approaches, flocks of homing birds come here for nocturnal rest; they twitter incessantly, as if all this pushing and shoving and brawling going on in their midst is for occupying the best branches. Goodness knows what restlessness compels a bird to leave one tree for another and then a whole flock to follow it. The branch creaks under the strain of this new load.

Matter of just one night, yet all this chatter.

Suvarna is lost in the chattering of birds. So much restlessness, such disquiet! Why not be happy with what is? There is Anant; she likes him very much, doesn't mind talking about him just anywhere. Today, again she told Ramesh, 'I enjoy talking with Anant; in the evening I'm going to have tea with him in the open park restaurant.' Ramesh's face paled a little; jealousy maybe, but why? He should understand that it is not possible for Suvarna to fulfil with him what she likes; not that it really is any shortcoming of his. Life is like that. Now, should Suvarna confine her likes to only those things that Ramesh possesses and get cooped up with them, absorbed to the exclusion of anything else? Suvarna has read how very negative jealousy is. She has always kept it at bay. Why, for no earthly reason, carry the baggage of a hurtful emotion? All this nonsense could pass muster in the days gone by. Then people had a lot of time; sitting idly, they could scorch themselves in the flames of jealousy. Today no one has time for such good-for-nothing things. So much is happening every moment; a vast expanse lies in front.

But how come Anant is with her and she is remembering Som ... as if getting acquainted with Anant, liking him and his company, all these seem to be pushing her towards Som.

Only three years ago, she used to have a tryst with Som, just like this. Difficult to live without each other. The moment he met, Som would seek privacy. As soon as he succeeded in his attempt, he would hold Suvarna in a bear hug. Som's ardour would drive Suvarna crazy. Som would even forget that Suvarna was the mother of two kids and older than him by three or four years. She would counsel him repeatedly, but all in vain. He was adamant; he would marry none but Suvarna. If they happened to reside in the same city, he would not tolerate her living with somebody else; he would commit suicide. Totally filmy. To be with Som was like being swept in a furious current. Not the slightest chance for thinking or using your brain. She was all along seeking to know whether her relationship with Som was impacting her life with anything positive at all.

There was nothing to gain except unbridled wildness, drunkenness. Som was used to uttering nonsense in his infatuation, and she, too, at times would let herself be carried away by intemperate thoughts. But soon she began to realize that all this was a sure-shot recipe for self-inflicted torture. Som's wish to marry her and all that ranting could be justified, but Suvarna's expectations from life were definitely not this alone.

Today she feels like talking about Som. Anant asks searchingly and Suvarna unhesitatingly reveals everything. Perhaps no relationship comes to an end completely. Its beauty, its sadness, its fun and frolic, they all become a part of you. It changes you; quite a lot does change. What's that which is here today but wasn't there yesterday, what's the difference between yesterday's Suvarna and today's, and what is that search that is leading her from one relationship to another?

'Are you still in touch with him?' asks Anant.

'He's in another city; keeps writing to me. I don't respond. I want to bring all this to an end, not so much for myself as for him. If I don't do this, he won't ever get going in life; he'll never marry. It's been more than one year since we parted company. During this period, he had been here too, but I did not meet him on the pretext of some work or the other.'

'You have amazing self-control. But have you ever thought how devastating within such restraint is?'

'Maybe. But was it sensible to continue that relationship?'

'What's sensible, what's not, I am yet to figure out. If you think you've done the right thing, then why do you feel sad?'

She didn't say anything, just began to tidy her dishevelled hair, sometimes straightening it, sometimes smoothening; but the strands were getting ruffled and tangled again.

'I was the first woman in Som's life, a novelty for him. I understood his feelings, so bore his overtures; but beyond a certain limit, it was sheer madness. To live like one possessed or to be actually mad, there isn't much difference between the two. Quite a few of my relationships didn't take off, or got snapped after reaching a certain point. People start crossing the line.'

'As for me, nothing beyond your face, neck, and shoulders have drawn my attention.'

'But in future it's possible you also reach that point when I'm left with no option but to break off. I've seen highly self-restrained persons getting carried away, and I had to treat them harshly.'

'I feel scared.'

'No, you needn't. If at all you appear to be crossing the line, I'll let you know.'

'You would come to know?'

'Yes.'

Suvarna began prodding inward – she wasn't wrong. Within her soft, warm exterior, she is very tough. This toughness she can bring into play whenever she wants to. She's drawn a circle in red around her and she doesn't allow anyone to cross it. Is it *Lakshman Rekha*? No, nothing of that sort. But there's certainly something within her that abruptly emerges hissing, soaks all her gentleness, and she becomes an altogether different person.

Deepak, too, went this way. Suvarna narrated his episode next to Anant. Deepak lived in the same locality during those days when she was in college. Suffering from the complex of his humble origin, he would write poems on Suvarna while keeping distance from her. He went over to Bombay to become a person of substance, but by the time he returned, Suvarna had become Ramesh's wife. Now Deepak had the confidence of being somebody and also those heaps of poems that he had written around Suvarna. Often she'd hear Deepak reciting them; sometimes she herself would read them in private. Those poems were brimming with the description of her beauty. The very thought that she could be an inspiration to somebody for poetic outpourings would suffuse her being with a feeling of warmth and pride. She felt sympathy for Deepak. At times she would wonder what could have happened if she had known before marriage that Deepak wrote poems on her. But now, at this point, there was scope for sympathy alone and nothing else, though she did not express it in as many words. He's adored her from afar for years, is still doing so, and hasn't married. She thought she would surely reward him some way, a little love, great respect, and heaps of sympathy.

So long as Suvarna featured in the poems and was compared to a fairy, she relished it. But Deepak's infatuation was heightening day by day. 'Stay with me tonight….Leave everything and come with me,' he even propositioned to this extent. At this point, Suvarna turned back.

It was a short story. Deepak was an incorrigible obsessive. Closeness with him meant always floating in the clouds, up above the earth, like something lighter than air. No scope for anything concrete. Of course, Deepak was free to wallow in such emotions; it was his choice. But to expect Suvarna to act likewise…? Life rests on concrete bases, to ignore them amounts to be knowingly foolhardy. Anything is okay so long as it makes life better, adds some positives to it. These airy-fairy antics, what can one gain from them except some titillation for just a while.

A sudden thought startled Suvarna. Anant too was a bachelor. Why did she always meet bachelors? Why would he be different from Som and Deepak? Can it be that she's cuddling up to Anant to forget Som, or to fill the void left after parting company with Som? No, had it been so, Suvarna would have felt satiated by now. But she is feeling with Anant the romance of striking friendship with a stranger, the freshness and expectancy of a new happening. Anant has something that she doesn't know, may not even recognize it on coming face-to-face with it. She wants to know, as though urged by somebody to do so, but she is a little subdued too. She doesn't relish getting involved again with yet another person. Would nothing else happen in her life except changing her romantic script with dazzling regularity – getting entangled with the second after the first, with the third after the second, then pulling herself away. The same sequence each time. Had there been something in it, would she have broken up with Som and Deepak like that?

Suvarna feels that there is something within her.... When it would come to light, it will fill up her entire life; she will feel complete, there would be nothing wanting. Then, without any self-doubts or qualms, she will be able to realize that she was born for this and this alone. She would no longer need anything from outside. What's that thing, what does Suvarna want, what ... ?

Baffled and restive, she runs helter-skelter, hoping that maybe here or maybe there, she will find it; this gentleman or that one will give her the light, which will show that invaluable but elusive something within her. Her quests come to nought. Every person with whom she develops some sort of affinity seems to have his own set of complexes that give rise to different kinds of complications inundating both of them and then sapping their energy and time in untangling them. Soon, the very feeling – when the doubt rises, are we going forward or not – itself dries up.

Suvarna knows this is what will happen. Yet she gets entangled with new people, as though she enjoys it, as if it's a sort of addiction. It's not just a matter of filling a void. She can remain occupied; there are any number of interests at her beck and call – reading, house management, taking greater care of children. She can start dancing again. Even if the new relationships do fill the void, this restiveness, this fidgeting refuses to budge an inch. What does she want to achieve, who is she running to, where does she want to go, what does she want to become?

The chirping of birds is on the wane. Whichever bough they got, they have settled down there for the night. Their abode is just for one night; our abodes for a whole lifetime. At dawn they will fly away. Human can't fly; does one for this reason remain stuck to whatever bough one chances to land on? No sooner does one leave it than he/she feels insecure!

We came out in the open after putting the birds to sleep on branches and boughs. In the midst of the bushes there was a narrow gravel path, dappled here and there with moonlight. The gravel crunched under our feet. In front was the lawn of the park, its greenery covered with the sprawling sheet of white moonlight. Walking slowly, we reached the lower end of the lane by the side of a roundish, bush-like tree. God knows what our eyes were searching in each other's, our lips eager to lick the wounds of the other. Her lips, reddish and full, were quivering like newly blossomed lotus on getting drenched in rain. This quivering of lips … like the flicker of a ray of light … the light of life … come get into me … come … come on … you come on.

We got into a tight embrace as if the other was the answer to the questions of the one – answers eternal.

'You being close fills me with confidence, Anant!'

'I chased you, caught you from behind.'

'No, I got you.'

'What would you call it?'

'Is it necessary to know, or give it a name? Whatever it is, is very good, very precious.'

'And when will that point come when my self-restraint begins to waver?'

'Oh!' separating herself, she began to walk on the path. 'You are stuck on the same groove. Don't bother, I'll let you know when it comes.'

'Only let me know?'

'No, I'll reform you too, hold you. Come, let's go.'

She is sad, feels like crying ... Suvarna said so on the phone. She sent for me. I felt elated. When I reached, I found her talking on the phone quite calmly and normally.

Not with Ramesh, nor with Deepak or Som. Her response on the phone, though brief, sounded quite informal, even intimate at times.

Is she as informal with the person she's talking to as she is with me? I cursed myself for my small-town mindset.

'Have you any work nearby?' she said after putting the receiver back on the cradle.

Work? I suffered a jolt. I hadn't come here on any work of mine. I'd come for her sake, on her asking me to come over.

'I mean if you have any business here, finish it and come back. Meanwhile, I'll get done with a meeting and return soon.'

'I haven't any work nearabouts.'

'Well, then wait here. I'll be back in no time.'

Without giving me a chance to respond, she collected some papers and went away. I picked up some old magazines and browsed through them, then made a few phone calls from her landline just to kill time. Recently, her room had changed. The pictures on the wall were new, but hung on spots similar to the ones in the previous room.

The instant I put the phone down, calls for her began to come one after another. Such a large circle she has, I wondered. I felt I was sitting in a crowded bazaar.

She returned after one full hour had gone by. Patting me on my back, she entered the room and instantly began to collect some papers.

I was feeling tired, couldn't even look at her properly because of fatigue.

'I'm sorry. Come, let's go, we will have ice cream. We'll just roam about.' Ice cream to appease a child!

While sitting in the car, I saw a magazine in her hand which she'd brought from the meeting. On the cover of the magazine was inscribed the name 'Shyam Mohan'. He was known to me. It was him she was talking to on the phone when I came here.

She was beaming from ear to ear. I was trying to locate the sadness in her, which she'd told me about on the phone. It was me who had come here to soak her sadness, but this gratification wasn't in store for me. Her sadness was now past history. Presently, it was poor me who was sad. She had intuited what was hurting me. But both of us were trying to avoid any mention of it.

We emerged outside. A mild drizzle had made the earth slushy. We were straining a little while walking. To one side were tall clusters of bamboo trees. During summer, the place has a cool ambience, but during rains it resembles hot peanuts soaked in rain, emitting steam. Across the grove, an ancient beautiful edifice came into view. I wanted to go in that direction. But Suvarna turned towards an ice-cream vendor. Despite the rain, she bought orange bars.

'Say something,' she said with mild irritation in between walking and licking the ice cream, but I couldn't utter a word despite my best effort. Our pace had slackened. We plonked ourselves down on a bench. I began to peep into her eyes. They were nowhere cagey. Can't I read her correctly, understand her? She took my right hand, placed it on her lap, and began to read the fate lines on my palm. 'Your heart line is inclined towards Venus and your lifeline too is raised quite high. See here. This means longevity. And you won't have any serious illness either.'

'Is having a long life an end in itself?' I said.

'Why not? I do want to live long.'

'What do you stand to gain? If there's nothing worthwhile to accomplish or achieve, what will you want to do with a long life?'

'That which I'm doing now.'

'In old age?'

'Then there will be different pursuits. Old age has its own charm.'

After a short rest, we resumed walking. We approached a big mausoleum. The main gate was in ruins, but the inside was fairly well maintained. Such a huge edifice housed only one tomb. There were steps to go up. I climbed a few steps. I extended my hand to help her. Holding my hand, she climbed two steps, but declined to go further up. The steps were quite high. She climbed down. I also climbed down behind her and just wandered around. That very moment she came from behind and almost swung on my neck. That touch … we were speechless. Some other sort of language had strung us together. Though not in a position to see her, I was lost in her. A trance-like state, lasting but a moment, at par with infinity.

Just an instant, but to be completely lost, where our separate bodies, our separate beings, had dissolved. Everything finished … we too … even the feeling that that moment we had elevated ourselves, we were non-existent. What happiness is it … surely not of this world, why doesn't this feeling come with just anyone? Isn't everything else meaningless before this ecstatic experience – who is she, who does she belong to, what is she, why is she what she is?

We were in the midst of ruins, but felt as though a flaming torch had landed in our hands in whose light even the ruins appeared beautiful. We were searching something that was hidden from our lives but was beckoning us.

We came out clasping each other's hands and were walking almost huddled close against each other.

'I am sure I can walk like this, my hand in yours, publicly, before anybody and everybody.'

Her eyes were assuring me, as if telling me, she isn't like others, not even as she seems to be. Understand me, read me right.

7 October 1977

Post-marital relationships in the Indian context: If they are wrong, then why do they develop at all? Do men and women get transformed into zombies after marriage, not amenable to forming new relationships?

Blissful experience … is it merely an illusion … a deception, as we describe any such feeling which is beyond our reach or which isn't a part of our recurrent daily experience? This is nothing but straitjacketing life.

What do I want from life … is there any purpose here or is passing time the sole aim? Then why, from time to time, the quest for meaning, why this restlessness, why does a faint shadow of sadness keep falling on even fully contented lives? Why does no one ever achieve perfect happiness? On the flipside, if we view life only as physical, then why do people, despite suffering, pain, and frustration, continue to cling to life … get up again even after harrowing accidents … is it merely because one cannot die … or is there some purpose to living … some moral compulsion … as though living is a sacred duty that cannot be cavalierly violated … what is it for which this self-devised regulation exists?

The heart longs for love. Psychologists tend to interpret it in several ways. They can even deem it a disease and suggest several remedies for it as well … but my heart refuses to be satisfied with such simplistic interpretations.

How is it that since meeting her, even my routine life has undergone a sea change for the better? Why is it that the sense of fulfilment I have after establishing rapport with her doesn't happen with anybody else?

All sorts of opportunities lie before me – I can be a highly educated person, a successful journalist … an intellectual … can head towards spiritual development and, if nothing else, can at least join the rat race for seeking pelf and power. Am I neglecting other important aspects of life? But this is bound to happen when you single-mindedly pursue a certain objective. If we don't do so, we are prone to chasing different pursuits and, at the end of the day, are left to wander about with partly quenched thirst. Then the pleasure of having achieved something or being someone is denied us. What will I achieve where I'm presently headed? Anything may or may not come about, but it appears certain that love, removing the debris of facade, brings to the fore our real self … is it any small gain?

Then the obsession to achieve or accomplish something in the context of life – this fantasy itself looks hogwash to me. Where everything comes to an end sooner or later, what can be called an achievement anyway? Since everything comes to an end, so maybe, every person dreams of some such thing that won't do so. For an ordinary person like me, this effort is reflected in the process of living … perhaps, in the midst of transience, love is the living image of our yearning for permanence. Viewed superficially, everything in love appears to be even more short-lived … but actually, it doesn't happen so. No doubt fulfilment in love may, in the measure of time, be temporary … but what a great deal it leaves behind … a great deal!

Tug of War

Just by the way it had been decided one day that I visit her house. 'Come, we'll have some drinks. I will also join you,' Suvarna had said.

'Ramesh doesn't forbid you?'

'What's there to forbid? I'm not a habitual drinker. Sometimes he himself makes a drink for me. A small peg with warm water cures sore throat, cold, and such other minor ailments. Do come, we will chit-chat.'

When I reached, they opened the door for me as a duo as if they were both waiting for me, were happy about my visit. 'Welcome,' Ramesh said, while it was writ large in her eyes. Ramesh received me in a gentlemanly manner. The alertness on his face that I had noticed when I had first met him seemed today to be his permanent fixture. Dressed in shirt and trousers, wearing polished, shining sandals, smooth-shaven face, and well-groomed hair … he looked smart.

While saying welcome, he bowed a little and his voice also had some extra warmth. When I had first come here, his voice had sounded normal, similar to while talking on the same pitch, neither high nor low. Today, evidently, there was warmth in it.

Ramesh sat beside me. To strike up a conversation, he picked up some latest news. Then we gradually drifted towards discussing the sociopolitical state of the country. I said, these days violence is pretty much on the rise. His response was that according to statistics, the incidence of violence in India was much less than in many other countries. Then the topic of policing came up. His point was that, according to the graph, crime had gone up parallel to the growth of population and unemployment, but the strength of police personnel had stagnated at the previous level. The gadgets to assist them were very old and almost obsolete, and the administrative structure and functioning was woefully antediluvian. To cap it all, pressure on the police force was increasing day by day. The police has to undertake all kinds of tasks, whether related or unrelated, and were held responsible for any incident. Everyone relishes censuring the police for the slightest reason.

Ramesh's manner and content of talk tallied with his appearance – commonplace and clear ideas, the very same that bureaucrats have, allowing no space for individual or out-of-the box opinions … depth of their beliefs just about matching their modulated low-pitched voices. An individual sounding more profound is liable to be dubbed an old fogey. The tone and tenor of our discussion resembled a locomotive, rolling evenly on its rails, and its level rose only at the point of analysis, yet sans emotion and ideology. All said and done, he was a meticulous person whose everything was always in place. You will feel good on meeting him, but only for a short duration. If you don't meet him, you aren't missing anything. Very soon I got bored. How much of such talks benefit us? If at all, there is only a very slight addition to our overall information, yet a rather large chunk of time of people of our class is spent on them. Maybe, this way we now and then like to convince ourselves that we aren't insensitive persons; we are quite thoughtful about our country and we do have some ideas of our own.

Ramesh was well informed. Career-wise also, he enjoyed a good reputation. Everything around, he felt, was passably good. And I in their midst.

'Well, what will you have – tea, coffee, soft drink?' Ramesh asked, as if drawing me out through his goodness.

'Ramesh, let's serve some drinks ....' Suvarna intervened in a very natural way. Till now she had been busy with sundries all over the house, leaving me with Ramesh.

'Okay ... what will you have, whisky, rum, gin?' Ramesh was quite proficient in Hindi, and so far had been talking in Hindi. But whisky, rum, and such are foreign liquors, hence perhaps his switching over to English.

'Thanks. I'll have rum.'

'Yes, in India we do make good rum, whisky just so-so.'

He went to a cupboard. The lower part of that polished, shining cupboard was used as a bar. Inside there were only four or five bottles, half empty ones at that. There were some glasses – different for beer, whisky, and wine. It appeared that the bar had been set up rather half-heartedly … the house must have this too!

Ramesh poured a little more than a large peg of rum in a glass and, with his back to me, asked, 'Soda or water?'

'Water, no ice.'

'No ice?'

'No restriction as such, but today I don't feel like it.'

Ramesh prepared only one glass and placed it before me.

'What about you?' I asked him.

'I don't drink.'

For the first time, I noticed a trait in him and, for that matter, everybody does have one.

'To me, every sip of wine seems to be the new line of a poem. A drink gives aesthetic pleasure, provided of course that the quantity is small….' Suvarna was impressed by this statement; even in the midst of the din and noise, she would not let the essence of a talk escape her.

Saying 'cheers' I started, but was feeling embarrassed. Here I was, drink in hand, taking small sips; and there they sat with a smile, watching me drink.

'Ramesh, please give me a peg too … feeling tired,' Suvarna said, signalling that she might join.

'No, you don't need it.'

'Ramesh, please.'

'No!'

Ramesh's voice was flat, but there was a sort of glow on his face, as though his individuality found fulfilment only in the exercise of power and authority. Like in office, he had taken a quick decision here and now stood firm on it. He had also made it clear that he was averse to his wife drinking before outsiders. While imitating the rich in various other things, here he was clinging fast to his middle-class mores. This was the second characteristic that had surfaced today.

Suvarna was sort of cowed down, and didn't press further. Neither did she let on that she was disappointed. Rather, with a view to interacting with us more actively, she drew the stool nearer and began to take a keen interest in the conversation, which she had so far distanced herself from. Now, fully diverting her attention towards me, she gradually began to introduce other topics in the talk – literature, drama, art, philosophy. Ramesh had no interest whatsoever in them, so he had to remain silent. That Ramesh might not feel neglected, I would time and again return to him, but Suvarna would come in the way by giving some fresh twist to the talk, and then we would revert again to our ongoing topic. A couple of times, I felt she was doing this deliberately.

Ramesh was now looking somewhat cut up. Then it dawned on me that flamboyance was not a part of his persona. The streak of authority he had, he owed it to his official position; it would erupt only on certain special occasions. One such occasion was just a little while ago, when like a perfect host he extended a warm welcome, the other when he forbade Suvarna from drinking. Both the occasions had gone by. Till a third arose, he had but to feel downbeat. He badly needed a role that would restore his self-esteem.

'Come on, have this now. You have been nursing the first for such a long time.' While I was chatting with Suvarna, he had prepared another glass that he plonked before me, while I hadn't yet finished the first. I had no inkling when he had got up and prepared it. When he himself was not drinking, his plying me with drinks as if I were a drunkard looked somewhat humiliating to me. I wondered how a person who looks so simple and cordial from outside could be so vicious within. Again, the peg that he had prepared was rather large. Was it his intent to see me blind drunk? I didn't pay attention to the glass and, as before, remained engrossed in talking. Irked at my lack of response, he crossed over to the record player and started playing a record of western music at full volume and came joyously towards me.

'Listen to this. Whoever listens once wants to hear it again and again.'

Our chatting stopped. I had perforce to listen to that record. I had an urge to get up and leave, but there was this blessed brimming glass to gulp down. Once it did cross my mind to leave the glass untouched.

'Please don't make any more drinks for me,' I had to check him beforehand.

'Is that all?'

Words full of sarcasm, as if he was taunting me – 'With all your macho posturing, you turned out to be nothing but a softie.' Or was he showing off his affluence and his magnanimity, though I was too low in status to deserve it.

Owing to tipsiness, I was all the more amused at his naivety. I was thinking that if I guzzled a peg or two more and began to swagger and stagger, he would be able to tell Suvarna, 'Look at this friend of yours, this is why I don't let you drink in public.' But if his motive was really on these lines, there was also the likelihood of some noxious thing being mixed in the drink.

The western music record had interrupted our discussion, which I couldn't relate to now thanks to that jarring sound, even though Suvarna was sitting before me just like before. So far I had been in a sunny mood, but now began to feel let down.

'I think I'll take your leave.'

'You didn't like the record. Seems that you are not interested in music? You ought to be ... it adds....' Ramesh observed.

She, too, appeared to be disappointed with me for the first time. I was expected to have little or more interest in all and sundry.

'I don't think music, art, or religion are mere hobbies, as if we added one more profitable thing to our lives and that's that. They cater to an individual's inner needs, impact us inwardly. This effect can be more or less according to our knowledge of music,' I explained.

'I have no knowledge of music as such, but even then Indian music does touch a chord within, somewhere deep down. But western music just goes over my head. You may blame it on my upbringing....'

'Your first view can be right, but no way the second one. Music is music. I'm as much moved by this record as Ravi Shankar's sitar,' Suvarna quipped.

'Why, disco these days! What else is it but crazy noise!'

'No, it has its own music. Music also changes with generations. Yes, to enjoy it, understanding is needed.'

The record continued to blare out. Nobody was listening to it. We were enmeshed in a discussion on the record and music, presenting forcefully every argument to substantiate our respective standpoint like moving pawns on a chessboard. Only a little while ago, Suvarna and I were chatting on topics that brought us closer, but now we were needlessly squabbling by countering each other. Ramesh was enjoying. Owing somewhat to my tipsiness, I was quite voluble and a tad harsh too. I could hear my own chattering. They were both on the same page.

'I think I will leave now.' Saying this, I got up abruptly. I didn't want to fall further in my own eyes. I finished the rest of the drink in one gulp, and then saying 'namaste', I came out.

'Ramesh, I'll see him off,' Suvarna told Ramesh at the door itself.

Ramesh stopped the record and got busy in arranging the bar. Closing the door after us, we came out in the veranda and proceeded towards the gate.

'Bored?' she asked.

'No, unnecessarily got involved in the discussion.'

'Why unnecessarily?'

'A discussion is an exercise in futility. It generates bitterness. Nothing is gained from it.'

'No, it isn't like that. We get to know each other's standpoint. Thus, we get an opportunity to weigh and test our own views. At times, a debate is good.'

For her everything is good … but for me, equally, everything is useless. Who is right … who knows? I was about to say something, but I noticed Ramesh walking almost at running pace approach us. Either he wanted to see the effect of the drinks on me, or he didn't want to take the risk of leaving his wife with a drunkard.

I folded my hands; they responded likewise. Behind Suvarna's joined palms, the same smiling eyes, twinkling like lamps. When I was about to turn round to leave, she affectionately hit my arm.

Evening 6.30. Ramesh is home for quite some time. Suvarna hasn't reached as yet. Before leaving the office, he had phoned her; she wasn't in her room. The office closes at 5, but it often happens that Ramesh reaches home and there is no one except the domestics to attend to him. Sometimes, even they aren't there. Boys away playing. Ramesh sipping tea, sitting alone in the veranda, browsing through the morning newspaper or some magazine. On such occasions, he strongly feels that a wife's domain should be her home. Husband returning after day-long hectic schedule, there should be someone to attend to him, to give him company.

At morning, a phone call had come in his office from one of his senior officers. Ramesh had met him; Suvarna had introduced him to the bigwig. His phone calls have been coming at home, but for Suvarna only. Today the call was for Ramesh. Curiosity arose in his mind, as also a bit of fear.

'Suvarna has invited me for lunch at 12 in her office. Join us.'

'Yes, Sir!'

Whatever the situation or matter, only a prompt, servile 'Yes, Sir' comes out habitually. Declining was a far cry, even giving some excuse didn't occur to him. Later, of course, he brooded whether some excuse could have been made. No, the senior would have felt offended.

Things would have been different if the bigwig had been invited by Mr and Mrs Ramesh, and he had gone to deliver the invitation, or at least Suvarna had made the plan in consultation with him. Instead, the information came from an outsider!

Ramesh reached on time. Besides the official, Anant was also there. He appears to be acquainted with the big gun. From the conversation, it transpired that Shyam Mohan was also coming. Suvarna taking the lead as usual, Ramesh on a chair at the edge, responding to only those queries that are directed towards him. If the queries are from the senior, his answer is extra courteous. This over-courteousness, however, pricks him when he sees that at that very time and with the very same person, Suvarna is chatting with confidence and in such a friendly, informal, bantering manner.

Shyam Mohan's phone call. He can't come, is busy. The people present here all belong to that class whose members know fully well what being busy means. What's the matter … he's used to coming post-haste at Suvarna's call. He might be desisting from coming, because he wouldn't occupy the centre stage today. No way will the senior let anyone else usurp that position.

After the lunch, all go down to see off the high official. Ramesh opens the car door.

'Ramesh, go with him,' Suvarna suggests.

Ramesh sits beside the senior. Suvarna and Anant are left behind.

When the car stops at the office, Ramesh quickly gets out. He makes a dash to the other side to open the car door, but by then his senior has got down. They were laughing and joking during the lunch, were serious in the car, and now completely formal. The senior, while offering thanks, shakes hands with Ramesh and enters his office. Not even once does he ask Ramesh to step inside for some coffee. Ramesh understands, this is all part of hierarchical culture. He too treats his subordinates in this offhand, snooty manner.

What was he thinking about? Oh yes, about wife and home. There was no need for Suvarna to join the service. When Suvarna said it was necessary for her, he didn't prevent her. But now the matter isn't just confined to service. Suvarna is more social by nature, Ramesh should appreciate. It will be uncivilized to say that he doesn't like Suvarna having so many friends. Suvarna's friends will also come to their house and Ramesh, even though he doesn't like them, has to sit with them, take interest in them.

What's it after all that Ramesh doesn't like? It annoys him no end as to why Suvarna has so many friends, why she is on intimate terms with some, why she doesn't keep herself confined to Ramesh's friends? The only sticky point is that his wife is beautiful and always surrounded by admirers, so much so that even high officials lunch in her office. In that royal court of hers, Ramesh's presence is that of a mere sidekick! Suvarna wants all sorts of friends – one poet, another artist, third journalist, the fourth sportsman, and so on. Her contention is that, thus sitting at home, she gets a view of those worlds. But what's the use of knowing them if you have to ultimately live in your world – Ramesh is unable to figure out.

It makes little difference if both of them live their ways, but then some disagreements do begin to crop up. Those few hours when husband and wife are closeted, if others were to occupy wife's thoughts? At times Suvarna returns home dog-tired; whatever energy she is left with, she spends on the children. At night when Ramesh would try to pull her to himself, then … 'Ramesh, please … I'm tired, had so much work.' Often she comes home complaining of a headache. As night sets in, she starts popping tablets. Looks like she keeps her best for outsiders, only the leftover for Ramesh.

The tea has gone cold. Throwing it away, he pours fresh tea from the teapot into his cup. The garden before him looks sluggish. The big creeper on the gate is still densely spread but withering from the inner side … has Suvarna noticed or not? It's she who looks after the garden.

Suvarna's car entered and, raising some dust, proceeded towards the garage. She is coming with quick steps. Ramesh watches her from the veranda. She comes panting, plonks herself down on a chair, and likewise drops the purse on another chair close by.

'How futile these evening meetings are … the time fixed will be 4:30 and then stretched for no rhyme or reason … the discussion will veer around trivial matters … Ramesh, can I have a cup of tea?'

'Didn't you have tea in the meeting?'

'That was at 5. It's now past 6:30.'

'Oh!'

Knowing fully well that Suvarna wants him to make the tea, Ramesh, without saying anything, pushes the tray towards her. There is already an empty cup awaiting Suvarna since long. Ramesh's pushing the tray pricks her a little, but she starts making the tea.

Suvarna's meetings … Shyam Mohan's business … Ramesh understands. If you don't want to meet somebody, just send word – busy in a meeting. The visitor has to believe because day in day out, just any time, with anyone, these meetings are on. Today, the very ploys that members of his clan employ were putting Ramesh in a spot. Suvarna's meeting could also be real or imaginary.

'You should return on time,' Ramesh's voice is cold, but it reaches Suvarna like the touch of a red-hot rod. She abruptly stops making tea, and turns a penetrating gaze at him. There was the stamp of authority behind the cold tone of that small sentence.

'In service, there is no scope for personal choice,' Suvarna's riposte was equally stern.

'Your job is not like mine requiring you necessarily to come late.'

'You seem to imply I myself don't want to be home on time.'

'I'm not insinuating anything, but there are other women also in service. How do they return home on time? Those who don't, they set tongues wagging.'

'I'm concerned with you, not with others; what you say, what you think. And you know I'm not like other women, I respect my individuality.'

As usual, the matter gets deflected there. Prickly silence overtakes them. Ramesh's grouse is that he keeps waiting. Suvarna's annoyance is that when she reaches home, she is greeted with sermons and taunts. For some time, both remain engaged with their cups of tea.

'Ramesh, you don't suspect me, do you? Your comments seem to suggest that I had gone somewhere else. You know well that I don't do things hidden from you. You know about all my friends. When I have to go with them, I let you know. Then why will I go anywhere surreptitiously? Where is the need for secrecy?'

'I wish we spent at least the evening together; for at night, I have to often go on duty.'

'That is my wish too … and this wishing is the real thing, not the time restriction you want to thrust on me. You know pretty well that I don't like such restraints.'

She gets up fuming. She combatively crushes any interference in some such way that Ramesh may begin to feel he is a nobody. Ramesh fails to reach anywhere. Not possible when Suvarna will always take her chosen path and Ramesh will be left behind. If, at all, sometimes both are required to walk together, he is dragged from behind as happened in today's lunch. Suvarna makes no bones about saying that she can't help if she has more friends than Ramesh and she enjoys outings and socializing, while he doesn't. Ramesh often feels that they are perpetually in the office mode. At home also, they are not husband and wife; they are just two colleagues. There are differences between them, heaps of issues likely to cause a clash, which at least he manages to keep suppressed and thus saves the day. If, however, a clash does come about, what have they got to convert the conflict situation into that of mutual friendship and love?

One complaint against Ramesh is that he doesn't take interest in household matters. Right from the very beginning, Suvarna's attitude has been to be in the forefront of everything and to have the final say … whether it's the colour of walls of the house or which plant will be kept where. As a result, Ramesh, too, is content to watch from the sidelines, leaving everything to Suvarna. She will manage somehow, regardless of whether Ramesh comes forward or falls back. As for Suvarna, no way can she help coming to the fore.

Suvarna goes into the bathroom to control her temper.

Ramesh's grievance has its genesis in the fact that he carries a fixed image of woman in his mind, has no stomach for any image outside this stereotype. He forgets that she is a working woman. Ramesh has no inkling whatsoever of the stresses and strains that are always present before her, whether at home or outside, such as coping with office tensions, looking after children, fulfilling social obligations, running the house, all at the same time. This multitasking pulls her in different directions. Nobody in the office should have the slightest chance of underrating her in comparison with her male colleagues, nor at home should Ramesh, her in-laws, or anybody else think that the household is being neglected, or the children feel that there is no one to look after them as their mother goes out for work. As for Ramesh, he has only his office to worry about. He doesn't even know how the house is run, where from rice is coming, when were the pulses last bought … and it's beyond him even to think that Suvarna is a separate individual, that she would have things and needs strictly personal, and she can also be thinking about her life, her fulfilment, her quest for completeness – things she can't spell out clearly even to herself, as yet.

She plays all the roles with great finesse. Where at all she slips happens to be the role of wife and that too because Ramesh is too much dependent on her. He is a simple fellow, so simple that he even looks dull and boring. He has no world of his own. After office, just home and children. He has hardly any friends. Even those who happen to be his were introduced through Suvarna. Ramesh can say that he loves her with his heart and soul. But after the birth of the children, the mere expression of love doesn't foot the bill. Ramesh has no interest in the children either. Leaving everything in the hands of Suvarna, he feels relieved. While at home, he will be poring over a newspaper. Quite often, he comes to the breakfast table, newspaper in hand, and then is off to office. As if interest in home is limited only to sleeping, eating, and newspaper reading. Wife to shoulder full responsibility of the house, do all the shopping, run the household, even to decide where and what decoration pieces are to be put up, which curtains to hang where. Whether the children go to school or not, what is to be done, if they are weak in any subject, all this too is the wife's duty, and he, the husband, while sipping the tea, grandly issues a diktat that she should be home on time. If Ramesh brings money to the house, so does Suvarna. Then why not share other responsibilities too equally? For the last few months, a vague question has begun to rise between them as to how much from each one's salary is being spent on the house. It's possible that it's an innocuous question and has arisen owing to the compulsion of having separate accounts in the bank. She does have the freedom to withdraw whatever amount she wants to from Ramesh's account, but why has she begun to feel diffident in telling Ramesh? Is it possible that both of them desire to keep maximum amount in their respective accounts? Family matters can be sorted out by mutual discussion. And they do discuss. Ramesh shows readiness to do whatever Suvarna wants him to. But when it comes to the crunch, things are back to square one. He reverts to his old fogey ways of passing everything on to Suvarna. All this shows a mulish streak in him. Suvarna often gets worried about the children's future. Ramesh has a formal sort of relationship with the children, and that too via their mother, not directly on his own. In such a set-up, which way will they be moulded, who will be their guiding light? No matter how much love she might shower on the children, can she fill the gap of a father's caring hand? At times, she's assailed by a scary thought that in such an environment the children are bound to have a feeling of insecurity. What will they do in life? She remembers her own childhood, how her parents took care of every single thing pertaining to her. She could never know what she got from which parent. Are her children getting even a quarter of what she had had from her parents?

Right now, there's an itch to bring about a change in the present state of affairs. When this also ceases to exist, then what? How strange is this chain of events! First there is the urge to be together. When together, a subtle struggle starts to get the better of each other – either she will make Ramesh soft as water or he'll turn her hard as stone.

No, Ramesh is a simple upfront person and these very traits are responsible for his troubles … gradually everything will be all right.

'Ramesh….' Coming out of the bathroom, she calls out loudly. Ramesh comes inside.

'Come on, dear! We haven't been to a movie since ages. Let's go for the night show. I'll rustle up a quick dinner….'

Paan Bahar

Suvarna looked at her watch and then made a call – 'It's me here.' Then, mostly monosyllables and exclamations from her side – 'Yes', 'Okay', 'Hmm', and so on, speaking less and listening more. Since I was sitting before her, she wasn't able to talk freely on the phone. Whoever was on the phone wanted to come early. Suvarna was in a fix and a bit fidgety. At last, in a low voice, she said, 'Ok, come.'

I had been sort of sniffing that for some time. Whenever I went to her office to meet her, I was bound to encounter the guy – who presently was at the other end of the phone – even without his physical presence. In my presence, she generally made few phone calls. But, of late, as coincidence would have it, whenever such phone calls were in progress, I would be around. Either when I reached there, a conversation on the phone would be taking place, or when I happened to be there, invariably a phone call would come. It even came to such a pass that whenever the phone rang, I'd have a telepathic feeling (maybe Suvarna too felt the same way) that it must be the same caller. And, in nine cases out of ten, it would turn out to be so, as if that fellow was keeping a close tab on me and knew that at that moment I was present there. If this guess of mine was wrong, another possibility could be that Suvarna and that person talked with each other not only once or twice but multiple times daily. Uniform pattern of talks, as if ice is melting gradually, and often the same concluding words from Suvarna, 'Call you later.'

Even though it was just the two of us there, thanks to this longish phone call, I had an uncanny feeling that a third person was lurking around somewhere close by. So, as soon as her call ended, I sought her permission to leave. I didn't want Suvarna to be put to any embarrassment. Not even once did she ask me to stay on. Instead, she got up instantly to signal a goodbye. Her lipstick-coated lips widened in a slight smile, her eyes in a melting mode. 'All right,' she said with alacrity.

As I was about to leave, she came close. In a flash, she embraced me and moved away after a quick kiss. An act lifeless, purposeless; nothing gained, nothing lost. No comparison of this robotic expression of love with those indelible moments I had had with her.

'Today you've smoked much less,' she was patting me, looking cheerful. 'Do ring up.' Her face lit up with a smile, one hand half rose to bid me goodbye.

I paused only after reaching the outer gate. Vehicles on the road … going to and fro … buses, cars scooters, taxis. Milling crowds … everyone looking alike, none with any individual identity. No one appeared to be going anywhere either, as if they were just being pushed to and fro.

Shyam Mohan's car was entering the building compound. Exit Caesar, enter Antony!

I had some acquaintance with Shyam Mohan. A middle-level officer, presently posted in the Secretariat, so a tad more important. A man of average build and much the same personality: nondescript, unremarkable. Cracks a joke at everything, as if nothing in life can shake him, because life itself is a big joke. He's fond of having girls around him. They lend sparkle, making every moment ravishing. No need to be particularly choosy. In his get-togethers, any girl would do. No matter if she isn't good-looking, so long as she is feisty and outgoing. But no way should she be a dumb doll, that's about it. The girls also hovered around him because of the position he was holding, high expectations of getting some work done or landing some job through his good offices. He, too, would find a way to help his protégés with shrewd manoeuvring. And here lay the secret of his wide circle of female friends. The assembled company at Shyam Mohan's place mostly whiled away their time in small talk and laughter and jesting, but assumed seriousness only when they spoke to him about their vested interests.

As in his office, so at home. Just a small family. No room for snarls or gnarls around the house. Wife on her job, son and daughter busy with their studies, all occupied in their own pursuits. Outside the responsibility of the missionary school for children's education, at home a tutor who coaches in turn the son and the daughter on alternate days. The servant quarter of the official house has been given to a family. The man sees to the work outdoors, while the woman works indoors. Shyam's wife is there to oversee their work. Having delegated and distributed work like a seasoned bureaucrat, Shyam Mohan is free to attend to his files and frolic. What was Suvarna's gain in having an intimate friendship with a person for whom everything was a plaything or a laughing matter? They would sit close on two sofas, where only a little while ago we were seated … perhaps Shyam at the same place where I'd sat. There would usually be found two empty coffee cups on the round table before the two sofas.

Today I was the last but one.

'Take the press conference report … I have nothing else for you … tomorrow will give you some matter … will the draft do? The second part after a couple of days.'

Sundry people coming one after the other. Suvarna has to pay attention to everyone, talk to them wearing a smile. A minister's press conference is an event. Because of the urgency of giving its report to the press, the post-conference time is very taxing.

People are coming and going, but Vinay is stuck around there … one moment he reads something, another moment looks for a phone number in the directory, then makes a call, watches visitors, or drags Suvarna into a talk, and sometimes only waits for Suvarna to be free from work.

A visitor from another city has no dearth of free time.

'Tomorrow I've to return by the morning train,' he said to Suvarna when the room emptied for a little while. His intention was obvious. He's been here for a day and half, but Suvarna's all along been busy. Today is the only day they can be together.

'Hi, Anant!' Cold welcome from her on Anant's arrival. Suvarna is a little irked. Just busy for two days and an army of friends descends upon you. Which is why she fixes time so that things can be organized, but at times this doesn't work, largely due to others. Anant also very much wanted to meet her today only. She had perforce to say, 'Come along. We'll leave the office a little early.'

Since the time Vinay has dropped in, all of a sudden, without prior information, Suvarna's been suggesting various activities for passing time – have you been here, have you been there, have you been to the noon show of that movie, it's very good … it will be taken off after the matinee – but the fellow seems determined not to take the hint. He just sits there, his gaze fixed on Suvarna – poor fellow. Maybe, he fears that once he goes, Suvarna will get busy elsewhere and it'll be difficult to get hold of her again.

Suvarna introduced Vinay to Anant and then got busy with her work. Visitors were trooping in one after the other.

'What's your programme?' The moment Suvarna was free, she asked Vinay in a frank and candid manner.

'Going back tomorrow morning.'

'Not tomorrow's programme. What about today?' Suvarna's tone was a little harsh.

'Today? Nothing today. Just to be with you.'

'Right now, I've to give Anant a lift. I'll be back home by 6:30. You reach there straightaway.'

'Okay! Meanwhile, I'll visit a friend. If it gets late there, I may not come … next time then.'

Vinay also unleashed the shock of a missile from his armoury. Suvarna didn't say anything and, as if unconcerned, began to collect her purse and other things to come out. He remained stuck there on the excuse of making a phone call, looking somewhat morose. Anant and Suvarna emerged outside.

'Wait a minute. I'll be back in a jiffy.'

She abruptly returned to her room as if she had forgotten something.

'Look here. We'll have dinner together,' Suvarna said to Vinay. 'Do reach by 6:30. I'll wait for you.'

She smiled and came out, pretending to put something she had forgotten inside in her purse.

'Day after tomorrow, on Sunday, my in-laws are coming,' she was telling Anant on the way. 'They desire to have vegetarian food cooked by me. I don't know how to cook veggie dishes. I'll have to go through recipe books. So much work here and no rest on Sundays either. This is sheer injustice on a working woman. Children's exams are also drawing nearer. I have to coach them. Then these meetings, seminar, and what not. Are they bent upon squeezing life out of me? But forget it. Good that we came out. I'm dog-tired. In your company I feel relaxed, can unwind.'

Outside Suvarna's car. Then towards the nearby park. I was thinking about the man left behind.

'He came at the wrong time … got disappointed,' I said.

'Who?'

'The one who was in the room … poor fellow!'

'I know, but how long for old times' sake?'

'Is he an old colleague?'

'Yes, he's a friend of Ramesh. Sometime back, he was quite a frequent visitor to our place. Then he was quite keen on me. Even when Ramesh got posted outside, he continued to visit. Subsequently, he also got transferred to Lucknow. He is still there. Occasionally comes for a day or two.'

'How far did the affair go?'

'Not very far.'

Her typical words in whose garb she could conveniently speak the truth, nothing but the truth. I went on probing further and further.

'Did you ever sleep together?'

'Don't be silly.'

'Anything else … kisses?'

'Don't remember … maybe once or twice,' she said, not batting an eyelid, while her face had an intense look.

'Must compliment you on your choice,' I said with a touch of sarcasm. I hadn't really seen any such thing in him that could impress a girl like her to let him come close.

'I never said I liked him. Can I stop people? I told you – this has been happening with me that they start liking me, and that too in next to no time.'

That moment, she turned out to be very ordinary. What was inside her that let her be available to any riff-raff, thus seeking pleasure in the mere fact that people liked her … and what was the complex that didn't let her affair with anyone cross a certain limit? Like a naughty girl knocking at a door and then running away … was she seeking gratification in the knowledge that so many were crazy about her? People should acknowledge her as beautiful, come to her court, praise her to the skies, and she free to keep everyone guessing. Or there wasn't any such pre-planning, just a couldn't-care-less attitude to have a good time with anyone she happened to encounter. Where does life give a chance to have someone after one's heart?

'I'd told you, perhaps ….' she added.

She hadn't told me. No knowing how many more such anecdotes are lying about strewn in some remote corner of her memory. Hop so quickly from one situation to another, from the second reverting to the first.…Will she…will she, by putting me aside, manage to relive the past with Vinay in the evening?

Tall trees in the vicinity, blue sky above, lush green lawn below. As if in a trance, she began to walk in the idyllic ambience, drawing in fresh air, as though extracting affinity from nature. If the company of males leads her astray, she comes to her own in the lap of nature. Howsoever much she may be tainted, nature purges her of the taint and cleanses her. Which is why she runs time and again to be with nature.

The hurly-burly of the office was no more troubling her, and Suvarna was feeling relaxed, rested. Now she just wanted to live the moments with me. We sat down on the grass.

'Is beauty a quality that grows all of a sudden – in some out of their laughter, in others out of their personal touch and sensitivity – or is it an integral part of their persona?' I was asking her.

'You talk big, but first tell me what beauty you see in me, how does it grow in me?'

She's always beautiful, excepting those moments when in trying to be logical or look clever, a sort of sharpness spreads on her face. Then she becomes petty ... feeling puffed up with pride on being complimented or rejoicing in the impression that people are 'keen' on her.

'Your beauty is intrinsic to your personality. It doesn't grow, it's there. Only it goes away sometimes for a little while.'

That moment, it dawned on me that I have begun to understand her gradually. Inside her, there is a flame of life that spreads in any direction. Inside me, there is just ash covering maybe a little fire, which has only the slimmest chance of being lit up from some outside spark, else it would stay put as ash. Her forte is to dazzle, mine to remain put out. Her type of dazzle also needed a particular type of cleverness – just being tactful, not a thinking type at all. What does she get out of pursuing frivolous pastimes and pleasures? Doesn't all this go on further splitting her personality? Maybe, she never paid heed to such thoughts.

An educated, cultured, beautiful woman, financially independent, she finds that all are eager to grovel at her feet; she also wants to explore, treat them her way and to whatever extent. Not only is there a sense of gratification for women's freedom after centuries-old bondage, but also the pleasure of running human affairs on her terms.

'I couldn't very much like any of your friends I met; all third-raters, including me.'

'I don't think so. Each one of them has something special, which may not be evident outside.'

'Ok! Is there anyone among your friends whose absence might give you unbearable pain?'

'Don't know. All such things are beyond me. Can't think on those lines.'

A layer of dust seemed to settle on my face. She was still in a predicament … something was gnawing at her insides.

'Perhaps, inside me is a cat, you know what. But it's an insignificant facet of my personality. My endeavour is to search for something better.'

'And you are searching it this way?'

'I think I am on a journey … I may chance to find it. Or I may veer round to the view that, whatever I am to get, I will have to find it only inside me.'

'This notion has been presented to us by any number of philosophers after pondering over it every which way.'

'But you do know that every person has oneself to seek one's salvation. Bookish philosophy is of no avail beyond a certain point. We all have our own crosses to bear.'

We are playing our respective games ... like two children who, even while playing together, are also absorbed each in his or her own game – one game together, another separately. I'm dying to play only with her. She plays, but every now and again, like the senior child, she chides me too ... 'Hush! Now don't look this side. Play your own game ....'

While returning, taking advantage of the solitude, I tried to embrace her.

'Shyam ... no, look ... someone may come, no Shyam ... no please.'

Not once, but twice she uttered Shyam's name. Even in such an intimate situation, if your companion is engrossed in thoughts of a third person, isn't it enough to devastate you completely? Shyam ... symbol of love! Radha seeks Shyam everywhere! For a few moments, I felt a bitter laugh rising inside, then felt shattered. She didn't notice anything, or all along was mentally somewhere else.

On the way back, she dropped me and, with a hurried 'bye', drove away.

Vinay was already there when Suvarna reached home. She knew that, despite her annoyance, he would come to her house anyway. He reached before 6:30. This happens with everyone; Suvarna has a hold over them. However, at that moment, she was ruing a little this wow factor in her. She felt somewhat irritated with Vinay too, but didn't express it.

'Hi, Vinay! Good you came. In the office, there's no respite from visitors. Hardly any time for friends.'

'Got rid of Anant?'

'I'll have a quick shower. Meanwhile, you go through those magazines.'

She dashed off to her room; sometimes there's nothing like being all alone. She flung the purse into the wardrobe and began to take out clothes for changing. Seeing a blue sari, she remembered that Vinay's favourite colour was blue. So she took out a blue dress and went into the bathroom. Out of habit, she kept humming a tune while bathing. No knowing how much time she spent in the bathroom … even if she wants to, she can't hasten her bath. She delights in the continuous spray of water on her body; it feels as if someone is running his fingers over her, caressing her. By the time she emerged out of the shower, Ramesh had arrived.

'Vinay has come,' Ramesh informed her.

'Yes, I asked him to come over for dinner. He will now have ample time to chit-chat with you.'

'But you'd invited Shyam for dinner tonight.'

'Oh no! How could I have forgotten that?'

'And I've invited Ravi.'

'That buffoon! What was the need?'

'One from your side and one from mine … I thought.'

'You couldn't find anyone else! Ramesh, please, sit for a while with Vinay. Let me get ready. I've also to give instructions for the dinner.'

Ramesh went away. Feeling at ease, she sat down before the dressing table to get ready. She could hear Vinay and Ramesh talking in the drawing room. She was just about getting the general drift of their talk, but not what was actually said.

Instructions to Ramu … chicken, dal, mutton mincemeat, two potato dishes, one fried and another with gravy, plain dahi, and also cucumber raita. Ramu grumbled, 'Had I known beforehand, I would have bought the things needed in the afternoon itself.'

'Doesn't matter. You can get them now. Two non-veg and four veg dishes have to be cooked. Since you're going to the bazaar, see if fresh fish is available.'

Ramu was sulking; Suvarna realized the slip-up, but she didn't get time to ring up home.

Impressive, but unnecessary, the ongoing conversation between Ramesh and Vinay! Just like the menu she outlined as mandatory for the dinner spread. As soon as she reached the drawing room, Suvarna made Ramesh get up, as if they were players in a game of kho-kho.…Just as the player tapped from behind with a shout of 'kho' stands bewildered for a second or two, getting his/her moorings, Ramesh kept sitting, probably with a view to quickly round off the point he was making. But Suvarna deprived him of the opportunity and peremptorily ordered, 'You are still in your office attire, go and freshen up.' Suvarna's final snub and Ramesh had perforce to go inside.

Not exactly the sort of opportune moment he had been seeking during the entire two days for an exclusive meeting with Suvarna, nevertheless Vinay grabbed whatever little came his way.

'I miss you so much. Do you even think of me?'

'Y-e-s!' Suvarna said, stretching the yes, her looks softening a little. 'I'm making a special dish for you. Haven't you looked at my dress. Blue is your favourite colour, isn't it?'

Vinay smiled in gratitude. He asked, 'You have many friends, don't you?'

'Yes, that's so. How about you? Made any friends there?'

'Yes, but none like you,' Vinay said wistfully.

It made her laugh. At that moment, Shyam and Ravi came in. Vinay's face paled visibly at the sight of these two. Suvarna rose to welcome them. Then followed the usual ritual of 'hi-ing' and 'hello-ing'. Ravi was a common friend, sort of. Little more than an acquaintance actually, but it was good enough for him to become informal with anyone. Then there was no stopping him and his no-holds-barred familiarity. Just as his shirt tucked inside his trousers would come out time and again, thanks to his flabby waistline, his off-the-cuff remarks directed at so-called friends would flow out from his mouth in season and out of season. Of late, the nearer his retirement age, the more voluble he had become, prone to laugh at almost anything and everything indiscreetly and indulge in self-praise. As if he was being ceaselessly tickled.

'So, Company Bahadur,' instantly on entering, he stepped towards Vinay and, after giving him a jovial slap on the back, said, 'Avadh evenings aren't suiting you, are they? So you've come on a tour of the old colony.' Without waiting for a reply, he strode towards Shyam and Suvarna, who, standing in a corner, were conversing in low voices. 'Now this is the problem. The twain meet and the world is finished; though not for us, only for you. I enjoy talking openly, not this hush-hush talk like a sticky substance. And Suvarna! When are you going to announce the new cricket team and who will you grant the honour of being the captain?'

'Ravi, can't you ever be serious?' she couldn't help being a little blunt, almost rude.

'Serious....? My dear lady, where to and where from? Who's serious, will you kindly tell me? Leaders of the country or officials, husbands and wives, fathers and sons, you or Shyam ... or Ramesh, who's serious? Pray, will I be honoured with a reply?'

'Well, for now, please be seated. I'll call for drinks,' Suvarna had to take this escape route.

They sat down on separate sofas. Ramesh came out to greet them.

'Hi, Mr Husband! Dear hubby. If one marries, the wife should be beautiful. Then there's always gaiety all round,' Ravi chirped again.

'Hello Shyam! How are you?' Ramesh shook hands with him.

'Good. How are you doing? Have you heard ... the Grand Lady is coming back?'

'You mean Mrs Gulati! Coming as what?' Ramesh welled up with curiosity. This was Shyam's forte, his USP. He always had prior information of postings in Ramesh's department, as if orders were issued with his concurrence. He would establish his importance by strategically revealing such vital bits of information.

'What a master stroke!' Ravi interjected. 'Where else will the Grand Lady sit? The seat for a she-elephant should suit her size and weight. By the way, Ramesh, have your detectives never tried to find out whether this putative Mrs Gulati has actually a Mr Gulati? I mean to say whether they actually got married … any proof … any witness. Photographs alone will not do. Lovers manage to get instant photo in a hotel room; lady love's hair decked with a floral garland. Baby Vinay! Why are you looking morose? Is it because your area is in the grip of a drought? But forget it … see, drinks have come. Pick up your glasses, gulp them down … then watch the river in full flow.'

Ravi began to laugh. Shyam and Ramesh were engaged in a serious discussion pertaining to Mrs Gulati's posting. Something hush-hush was going on between the two. This was evident from their serious faces. Suvarna was busy laying the table. Ravi volunteered to put soda and ice in the glasses.

'You won't drink, will you?' Ravi asked Ramesh. 'I don't think the wicketkeeper will have any. And you, Shyam? My dear playboy, you're sure to have because you can then immediately assume a different role to suit the occasion. What about you, baby? Quarter … or may I make it half? Come on, be bold.'

'I'll help myself,' Vinay said quietly.

'What else would Humayun do? Born in Kumayun, die in Badayun.'

Now Ravi turned towards Suvarna. 'Madame, will you just watch from the sidelines your Tajmahal or Tashmahal? How about tasting a few drops of … ?'

'Thanks. I have already made my drink. Here, buttermilk,' saying this, Suvarna sat beside Vinay. Pointing towards Ramesh's direction, she asked, 'Can you make out what they are talking about?'

Dismissing her question, Vinay moaned, 'Couldn't meet you in private….'

'Next time….' Suvarna said in an undertone and then hurled a sarcastic question at Shyam and Ramesh, 'Is it still Mrs Gulati….?'

'No, we were deliberating how far India should interfere in the affairs of its neighbours.'

'I know … if Russia can do it, why not we? Are we any less than a superpower? Vinay, what do you think?'

Ravi handed over their glasses to Shyam and Vinay. He raised his glass and said, 'Cheers, gentlemen!'

'A lady is also present here,' Vinay said.

'Really? Oh, come on, she isn't drinking, so….'

'Vinay, do you also, like others, consider India a starving and weak country?' Suvarna asked.

'No, this isn't the issue,' Vinay began seriously. 'At the end of the day, what it all boils down to is culture.'

'May I ask what you mean by culture?' Shyam and Ramesh directed their attention to this topic.

'Whatever is opposite of science is culture,' Ramesh said.

'No,' Vinay countered. 'Things that you can see, you can touch – this glass, house, job, wife, if all these things are snatched away from you, then what's going to sustain you despite this deprivation is culture.'

'Wow!' Ravi leapt at this. 'What a fine yarn you have spun, sonny boy! But the million-dollar question is whether the parade that takes place on the Rajpath every year on 26th January is culture.'

'Ravi, with you there, no discussion can reach its logical end,' Suvarna couldn't help expressing her displeasure.

'Who can ever reach where, Madame? You yourself haven't reached anywhere, have you? This is just empty talk. The bigger issue before us is feeding our hungry millions rather than becoming a superpower….And every time our neighbouring countries contrive to stir up violence within their borders and push a large chunk of their population into India. How clever of those blokes!'

'Ravi has come out with a real clincher,' Ramesh was unstinting in his praise.

'How can this be stopped in the prevailing environment?' queried Shyam.

'Such as how can man meeting woman be stopped? Aren't I right? Superpower! My foot! My dear wineglass fraternity, along with the talk, also focus on your glasses. Our madam-hostess is famous for being a stickler for time. Very soon she is going to proclaim to the accompaniment of drumbeat. Food is ready. Eat and get lost....' Ravi rapid fired his usual volley of inane comments.

'I'll check up on how soon the dinner will be ready,' she said.

'Didn't I say so?' Ravi said in a self-congratulatory tone, and forced Shyam and Vinay to gulp their drinks. Then he made fresh ones and placed the glasses before them.

'I'm seldom wrong, your lordships!'

'Ravi, do you find every discussion a hogwash,' Shyam asked him seriously.

'Of you fellows, certainly.'

'If a discussion between intellectuals is nonsensical, then....' Vinay complained.

'Yes. It's intellectuals' only that is nonsensical.'

'Then you too are a part of it,' Shyam retorted.

'This intellectual tribe is proliferating like the blessed cockroaches. Anyone with a smattering of English struts about as an intellectual. By mistake, I too fell in bad company and am finding it difficult to break off from it. And Madam looks in a kindly way at the whole world, but never at poor me.'

Laughter rumbled in the room like a sudden breeze. Even Suvarna, who was standing by the dining table, could not help chuckling. The party was now warming up.

'What do you think about this match India won against West Indies? Was there any match-fixing?'

'No. This fixing business is confined to politicians who strike a deal to go separate ways.'

'Are there any chances for the Lok Dal and Jana Sangh in the elections?'

'Why does India lose to West Indies?'

'Russia is not going to stop at Afghanistan, mark my words.'

'Films starring superstars are getting a beating. It augurs well for the future.'

'Action and stunt not catching the cinemagoers' fancy, stardom losing its glamour … most welcome change.'

'Our country is adept at making or breaking Janta Party-like coalitions. Can't something different happen here?'

'With good-for-nothings like us being there….' Ravi chortled.

'You are never serious even for a moment. Had you been, you would have seen that all of us are seeking redemption.'

'Yes, nirvana of Buddha or moksha of the Gita!'

'There's no moksha in the Gita. Its core principle is performance of duty without desire for reward. Lord Krishna has said… '

'And existentialism? It's also about this. Today's *Hamlet*! Can we say we're happy?'

'Why do you say we are not?'

'Yea, children are sleeping there. Food is laid on the table.' Ravi sings – '*Hum the, tum the aur sama rangeen….*'

'I don't see any reason for complaint. If we don't enjoy today but keep thinking only of tomorrow, we can never be happy. I think….'

'Do you know what's happiness?'

'Why not? What we are right now … that is happiness.'

The discussion kept warming up. Every kind of topic, every type of argument, about the whole world – from individual to national and on to international. In the meantime, Ravi had guzzled four glasses. Shyam and Vinay were wary after two. Ramesh was busy scraping information about Mrs Gulati from Shyam … who is backing her, what's the secret of her returning to the capital so soon after being sent out?

Dinner was announced. Shyam and Vinay drained off their glasses and sat down at the dining table. Ravi cussed them, prepared one more for himself, and brought it to the table. Still more varied subjects were coming up for discussion – Borg–McEnroe rivalry, possibility of a world conflict, weapons of Pakistan, dismissal of Railway Board Chairman. While gorging themselves with mince meat and mutton dishes and other delicacies, their table talk was mostly composed of stuff dished out by cheap general knowledge books.

'Ravi has had a drop too much,' Suvarna said to Ramesh.

'Such excessive drinking isn't good for his health,' Shyam added.

'Why don't you advise him not to?'

'Does he listen to anyone?'

'What will happen to him?' Vinay was worried.

'One day Shah Jahan's begum Mumtaz Mahal told the emperor that they hadn't tasted gravy made with gram,' Ravi in his groggy state was rambling.

'Ramesh, quickly finish your dessert and escort Ravi to his house. He's had his fill. By then, others too will have finished their dinner,' Suvarna said.

'I'll drop him,' was Shyam's generous offer.

'No, no … Ramesh will do it. Ravi stays close by,' Suvarna said.

Somehow, Ravi was made to have a small amount of the dessert and induced to get up.

'Okay! Will take your leave. Sahib bahadurs don't like Hindustani at all. See you again. Okay baby … Bye Shyam … thanks Suvarna … Ramesh … oh. You're coming with me.'

Shyam also got up soon after Ramesh and Ravi had left.

'You don't rush. Finish your meal at leisure,' Suvarna told Vinay. 'Meanwhile, I'll discuss something important with Shyam. My deputation file is under consideration.'

'One of my files too….' Vinay was petulant.

'You can discuss it later. Right now I want to talk to him in private. He has to leave early,' Suvarna was blunt.

Vinay's face dropped. Shyam and Suvarna went out into the garden. There was the mild moisture of dew in the garden and the solitude of midnight.

'Creates a scene, this Ravi. Why did you invite him?'

'Ramesh invited him. God knows why Ramesh likes this chatterbox,' Suvarna said.

'And this fellow from Lucknow?'

'It's so difficult to shake him off. An old friend of Ramesh. Comes for a day or two. Ramesh never fails to invite him for lunch or dinner.'

'Quite an odd sort of fellow,' Shyam quipped.

Shyam and Suvarna began to walk, their bodies touching each other. At that very moment, Vinay came out in the veranda and shouted from there, 'Come back. There's a phone call.'

'Who is it? Couldn't you ask?' Suvarna asked loudly.

'Phone.'

'It might be a wrong number. Who was it?'

'Phone … phone….' Vinay went on repeating.

'Idiot!' Shyam mumbled, and then said loudly, 'Tell him there's nobody at home.'

'No, ask the caller to hold on. I'm just coming,' Suvarna quickly intervened.

Further down was a cover of mango trees. They descended into the darkness. Shyam wanted to hug her. Suvarna didn't resist, her face suffused with mellowness. But the very next moment, she yanked herself from his clasp and stood aside.

'Ramesh, what are you doing here?'

Ramesh had come from the front gate; perhaps he'd parked his car outside itself.

'I was checking whether the mango sapling planted by me got crushed by mistake, while I was taking the car out this way.'

'Vinay said there's a phone call. Go check. Late night calls are mostly for you.'

'Darling, it can be yours too. Anant, big boss … you go and check. I'll see off Shyam. If the call is for me, say I'm not at home.'

Suvarna said bye to Shyam and went away.

Vinay was in the veranda, fuming. When Suvarna was crossing the veranda, Vinay pulled her into a corner.

'You didn't spare even a little time for me?'

'What can I do, Vinay? Press conference! That's why I want to leave this department and go on deputation. When you come next, all this hassle won't be there. Let me attend to the phone call.' Suvarna wanted to get out of the present situation.

'Must be a wrong number.' Vinay began to pull Suvarna towards himself.

'Vinay, what are you doing? Leave me. There are servants around. Does it look nice?'

'They won't come, they understand. You never managed to find time for me.'

Vinay dragged Suvarna to himself and planted a quick kiss. From outside came the sound of a car starting. Suvarna freed herself, pushing Vinay away and went inside.

Quite a few days had passed without any contact with Suvarna. I wanted to give her a call, but before this wish could turn into an urge, something or the other held me back. Everything is in disarray again. I continued to carry the burden of my emptiness, which I was accustomed to do for years. Neither did I receive any call from her – might have been saddled with heavy workload or pestered by an unending queue of visitors.

At long last, her phone call came.

'What happened? Long time no see. No news either. Have you been out of station?' she said.

'No.'

'Anything troubling you?'

'No.'

'But it does seem something is amiss.' Even when not face to face, Suvarna guesses right.

'Maybe something trifling, nothing much to worry about.'

'Why not to worry about? Am I the cause?'

'No. We are generally troubled owing to ourselves.'

'Will meet?'

'No.'

'Didn't want to ring up either?'

'Yes.'

'Could you come today?'

'No. Right now I want to grapple with myself.'

'Look....'

In that small word, how much empathy had surfaced, how much concern! Strangely, what she's able to say on the phone, she's unable to say when face-to-face with that person. It seemed she was about to cry.

'I'm dying to talk about many things with you. You're a very very dear friend. It's only you I can confide in, in whose company I feel so relaxed. Come, won't you?'

I was made to feel special. Now it was difficult for me to refuse.

When I reached her office, there were some people with her. The instant she saw me, her eyes lit up, as on recovering something lost. Quickly, she disposed of the visitors.

'We'll go out. Here, there's no stopping these fellows.'

She got up and began to collect her purse and sundry other things. Just when we had reached the door on our way out, Shyam Mohan entered. Coincidence! Straight out of a film!

The usual exchange of pleasantries. Shyam's sudden appearance made Suvarna's face go a shade darker.

'Come,' saying this, she turned back, moving around the table, reached her seat, and made a phone call for three coffees. How often we have to use small things as a cover to hide ourselves.

What a small world! The same people buzzing within a narrow circle, situations too, by and large, remaining just the same. The other day I was in Shyam Mohan's situation. Tomorrow could witness the repetition of history of him exiting and me entering. Then we'd managed to save the day. Today some invisible power made a mockery of much flaunted human ingenuity. Even then, the situation had gone amiss only marginally. We three could have sat together for coffee, and chatted while sipping coffee. But Shyam Mohan wasn't in a mood to tolerate – not so much my presence as our leaving the office to go out together. He didn't sit down; kept standing with his hands on the chair, feeling lost, his face flushed with tension. He made a feeble attempt to explain that he'd come here looking for somebody. Soon, under the pretext of some important work, he left.

Suvarna's face hadn't yet regained composure. I had, however, remained normal. Frankly speaking, I was deriving a kind of pleasure from the present situation: for today, I was inside and Shyam Mohan outside. Had I been in his place, I'd have fared worse.

'Let's go ....' She said as soon as Shyam Mohan had left, trying to gloss over the disconcerting situation.

'Coffee?' I reminded her.

She picked up the phone to cancel the order, and instead changed the order to two cups instead of three.

'What are you thinking?' She looked at me.

'The very same that you are.'

We both were really thinking about the one who had just left.

'Shyam Mohan looked troubled,' I said.

'Yes, but I can't make out what's eating at him.'

She doesn't understand these obvious things, or, if she does, she keeps on rejecting them. Maybe she's above all such things, but then why had her face darkened?

'He knows about you, that we're friends and meet quite often,' she said.

Old wives' tale! The heights that we manage to touch ... will it be simply labelled as friendship? Two males make better friends, they have better understanding ... then why can't they rise up to those heights? 'Friend' is a flexible word, hence quite convenient for today's shrewd man. No doubt we were friends, but only to the extent the element of mutual understanding between friends was mingled in our love. Maybe for her, our relationship is merely friendship. But then, when I begin to cross the limits, why doesn't she hesitate, object, or restrain me? Undoubtedly, nobody can take liberties with her without her consent. She has given me liberty only up to a certain point and not beyond; she had restrained Deepak and Som as well at pre-fixed limits.

'Have you ever realized how much are you strained this way? This split personality, leading a life with fast-changing roles daily … have you ever thought how this harried and hurried existence impacts your life?' I said while having coffee.

'I don't think so. Where is the split personality in this? Couldn't tell you before, I was a little troubled. Don't know why this happens to me. It's difficult for me to stop people … I haven't the heart to cause pain to anybody.'

'This happens with beautiful girls. Everyone seeks their company, though with different motives. But how do other girls not succumb to such overtures? And you too don't let them cross the red line.'

I was pontificating about her affairs as if I were her guardian. Possibly, I had, all of a sudden, assumed such a role so that I could reassure myself that I was more intimate with her than Shyam Mohan … but was I really so?

'When you talk of not causing pain to others, won't you cause pain to someone or the other if you go on being intimate with all?'

'How do men have several close friends on identical terms?' Her tone had both sharpness and sarcasm.

'That is a matter between man and man, not between man and woman where emotions do come invariably into play.'

'Why at all should they … why was Shyam Mohan so rattled? I'm not somebody's property, yaar!'

She suddenly flew into a rage. She was an educated woman, self-reliant, and capable of fending for herself, while people were standing there with ropes to bind her and pull her towards themselves. She might allow some such privilege to her husband, but how dare the remaining lot claim the same status!

'Look here,' she was saying. 'I insisted on calling you here. Today when you aren't in a good mood and somewhat disappointed with me as well, let me tell you plainly that you have to take me as I am. If, however, you really think that this will be difficult for you, then this is the moment we part. There will be a great deal to cherish what has gone by. After all, we've passed some memorable moments together. As for me, I consider those moments very precious.'

On phone she had been so affectionate, but here she was imposing condition after condition, like we were two traders negotiating across the table to strike a deal. See matters straight … logical discussion … part gracefully, quite a lot to cherish … but then where is the need, if anything, for it? Take her as she is … this can be feasible for Ramesh who has to live with her, come what may. But somewhere or the other, love does have an input of idealism, which is why it has the power to gravitate …

it propels the relationship forwards rather than letting it remain static by mere bonding.

'Today I want these matters to be discussed frankly. If either of us feel that we're just going through the motion of friendship, the best thing is to part. Why let it drag … this beautiful relationship that has gone so well all these days?'

'What do you think, can we have intimate relationship with several persons simultaneously, or knowingly or unknowingly form a new relationship to snap some old ties?'

'And why can't we do it? Every relationship comes with a different shade. If life gives an opportunity to build such relationships … spurning them is not only dishonouring life but also sacrilegious.'

'Ramesh must be feeling aggrieved when you go on forming relationships one after the other?'

'Why should he? I give him a lot. He could complain if I snatch something legit belonging to him and give it to someone else. I don't do anything at the cost of Ramesh or my home. But what can you do when Ramesh's needs are so few and I have so much to give…?'

'Can one love several persons at the same time?'

'Every relationship needn't be termed as love. Neither do I want love. Got a lot of it right from college days. All and sundry wanted to love me. Now I'm in search of a friend. You can make a good friend who you can confide everything to and get solace. Love leads to needless tensions which don't do any good to one's life, while in friendship there's ample scope for mutual give-and-take.'

Can life be viewed in this profit-and-loss account mode … I was wondering … love is useless because there are tensions in it, but the criterion for assessing the worth of everything is how much it adds to or subtracts from life.

'Your comment about my forming a new relationship to replace an old one … there is nothing at all of that sort. I don't initiate anything. At times I feel strongly that there's nothing but haze within me … don't know what I am and what happens to me.'

Very often, this male-oriented society appears to Suvarna like a marsh overfilled with mud … lush green from above but just one notch below slippery moss, mud, and slime … heaps of all sorts of rubbish. No sooner does she put her feet on the surface with great confidence than they get sucked into the treacherous swamp. An irritating stickiness engulfs her. At the end of the day, every man's sole effort is to possess her. Shyam is a good person, older than her by fifteen years. She thinks it is sufficient for Shyam to be by her side, chit-chatting over a cup of coffee in some restaurant on topics like yoga or politics, some day Suvarna shooting an admiring glance at Shyam, sometimes letting him do some risqué bantering, that's all. What does Suvarna lose if such occasional meetings can make a man feel young despite his age? That said, how can Shyam think that Suvarna should spend time only with him?

This Anant … innocent like a flower that fell on to her lap. Gets ruffled over trifling things and then broods about them needlessly. As though the building blocks of his personality are these very complexes. Honest to the core about his complexes. Even while trying to cope with them, he's able to generate vibes that give Suvarna a glimpse of what she hadn't thought of or seen before. In his reckoning, Suvarna is not just a woman; she is an individual in her totality. This attitude of his elevates her. She's often felt in Anant's company that she is a veena on which Anant can play myriad tunes. Thus, that facet of Suvarna's is coming to light that had hitherto remained concealed. She is not simply what she appears to be.

The world that Anant talks about is beyond her. Often, that world is out of Anant's reach too, but the very awareness that some such world does exist makes life so very meaningful. The intimate relationship and its uplifting experience that Anant talks of does motivate her to do likewise, but it doesn't come about. On seeing Anant, she sometimes feels how easy it is to let life go haywire and how difficult to keep it on an even keel. How easy to live in this materialistic and mundane world, but the world founded on philosophy and pipe dreams and supposedly within reach is, in fact, so evasive. Moreover, her own life seemingly so settled and secure – marriage, service, children, creature comforts – is in reality so unsettled, while conversely, Anant's life, apparently in disarray and rudderless, is so composed and serene within.

Sometimes she's scared of Anant. The way he sees and speaks ... uttering every word feelingly and losing himself in it. In such moments, she feels her entire being melting, the delicate warp and woof of emotions makes her shiver; it appears she's becoming a captive – captivity of emotions. If she slackens her hold on herself, she will fall a prey. According to American women, love is the greatest male conspiracy. How strange that despite being totally different from Shyam, Anant also thinks on similar lines, the same possessiveness. Only his tutelage, but why?

She was pulling her hair … highly distraught, free woman … yet helpless, despite all the props of intellect!

'You'd taken the responsibility of restraining me from committing any indiscretion … last time also, you'd rescued me. All misgivings had been removed that day, but today, treating me as a rank outsider, you have been raining abuse after abuse,' I couldn't help protesting.

'Difficult to do always, I too can desire sometimes for somebody to take care of me.'

Her big eyes … almost going teary … eyelashes fluttering like drenched wings. We were looking for ways to take care of each other. But neither of us fulfilled the condition of absolute dedication required for it. Our egos were the stumbling block. She was already in an indignant mood, but I don't know what constraint was holding me.

'Many a time I've thought of telling you – the morass I let myself get bogged down in,' she said in a subdued tone.

Several kinds of pricks and scratches surfaced on her face. Her face taut with anguish was looking so innocent.

Why couldn't I get involved with somebody else after she came into my life? Perhaps, she fully filled my emptiness, while I've filled hers only marginally – if at all. It must have been my shortcoming.

'How about going out?'

'Not today … some other day. If you want, I'll drop you home.'

She left me near my home. While leaving, she smiled drily and said 'bye'. 'Give a call' – she didn't say so this time.

Her fast and fiery analysis as a saw for dissection of life and, in between this, her helplessness dripping drop by drop, varied hues of emotions spreading on her chiselled face.

Spring was at hand. Her complexion was gradually glowing more and more by the day.

On phone she is sweet as usual, but when I propose going out somewhere in the evening, she postpones for the next day. Next day, an early call from her – she's suddenly got busy. The programme is further postponed by two or three days, and on that day too, prior confirmation required. Accordingly, when I called up, some other excuse was given. This way her procrastination went on for a number of days. When my eagerness to meet her refused to brook any further delay, she condescended. 'You may come right now.' When I reached there, the regal court was in full glory. She was having tea with her peers and acquaintances, interspersed with chit-chat on just any topic. Barb-like arguments clashing like arrows shot from opposite directions, punctuated with noisy approval or disapproval from the listeners. 'Hi Anant!' She introduced me to the assembled visitors. We exchanged pleasantries perfunctorily. Each and everyone puffed up and wallowed in their own importance. Suvarna's face was alight with a smug expression. She seemed to be in no hurry to get rid of the ongoing frivolous activity. Tired of all this, when I rose to go, she didn't stop me either. 'Okay! Bye! See you.'

When this happened the next time too, I was jolted into awareness. Then I realized that all these days, she hadn't made a phone call on her own. If at all she did, it was to convey the cancellation of our mutually agreed programme of meeting. Next time, to break her defence, I went to meet her without prior information. She wasn't in her room. To pass time, I picked up a magazine and began to turn its pages. I chanced to lay my hands on her engagement diary kept near the telephone. Her official engagements were entered against some dates, mostly formal meetings. Today's page was blank. First page had 'IMPORTANT DATES' marked in her hand … my birthday too was included with a small 'A' marked against it. There was one name referred to with a solitary 'S'; must be Shyam's. In the morning, when Suvarna wishes somebody a happy birthday with great ardour, how overjoyed that person at the other end of the telephone must be feeling that despite a maze of dates round the year, she remembers his date of birth. How simple a device to make somebody feel special.

Lest some such other thing come my way, I pushed away the diary. She came soon after and looked busy. She gave me a quick 'hi' and the next moment, picked up the phone and sent for her subordinate. 'Sorry. When did you come? I've to prepare a reply to a parliament question. I'll get some tea.'

I asked her not to. When I said I would go, she didn't stop me but only said, 'Awfully busy these days.' It occurred to me that there was a pattern in what had been taking place between us for the last two or three weeks. There must have been some deliberate plan behind it. She wants to change our relationship from 'special' to 'common'.... Or was trying to free herself from fetters that she'd unwittingly let herself be chained with. Who knows she might be dishing out similar treatment to her other friends too.

There's always a tin of *Paan Bahar* on her table these days. From time to time, she puts a spoonful in her mouth and keeps chewing. Her visitors also use the same spoon to put the granules in their mouths. She pushed the tin towards me too. 'Dirty habit,' I objected in a low voice.

'What's dirty about it?' She was surprised.

I didn't want to say anything more. While returning, I was wondering – no comparison between two lovers eating with one spoon and this sharing the granules with all and sundry using the same spoon.

22 July 1978

We are on the verge of separating. When we will, a big void will appear in my life. Nothing of this sort will happen in hers. She already has such small or big voids, which sometimes get filled and sometimes not; that's why she neither gets elated in a favourable situation nor depressed in an adverse one. In her world, the winds blow – sometimes towards 'A' and sometimes towards 'B.' On top of it, she doesn't relish revealing her weakness. If somebody is quitting, she won't chase him, rather she'll dump him into the backyard of time. After an interlude, either he'd have gone away or would have come back on her terms to savour her favour. Come what may, she'll retain her supremacy.

Quite a healthy attitude of today's lifestyle. Each man for himself!

I must ungrudgingly concede that she's independent. This signifies the modern educated woman's revolt against the age-old conceit of man that he's woman's undisputed lord. Her heart isn't a territory to be ruled by a single person. Conversely. why shouldn't three or four persons' hearts be her colonies where her flag flutters triumphantly? But there's one hitch here which is endemic in any sort of imperialism. She won't be accepted in toto anywhere.

In between other papers in the table drawer, a letter-like sheet – looking jaded and forlorn, handwriting familiar – Anant's. Suvarna picks it up.

Suvi,

I have no intention of going into the whys and wherefores of what I have gone through these last three or four weeks, nor am I giving or seeking any clarification. From your side also, nothing of this sort is likely to happen, because in your thinking there is no room whatsoever for critical introspection. What I have felt these days, how I have suffered lately – have been tossed like a leaf caught in storm, about to fall any moment – if I don't think about all this, I'll be unfair to myself.

One day you had said, 'We belong.' These two words speak volumes if only anyone could measure up to them, but did this happen with us? While you are so special in my life as to be the only one, unless I be the same in your life, won't 'we belong' remain an empty rhetoric? Maybe, my wanting to be special to you must have been behind my restlessness; this wish is not because of any distinct trait in me but because I feel that for you. Maybe just an instinctive urge on my part, but you … you find it convenient that our wheels move separately. At any chance meeting, we may have some give-and-take, then about turn and we go our separate ways. I want to be familiar with everything of yours, but mere mention in our conversation of any of your friends appears to be embarrassing and irrelevant to you. You do not like any interference from me in other aspects of your life, while I am keen to lay bare even my smallest matter before you.

Where a duet is contemplated, both the instruments have to be strung and tuned in perfect sync, be attuned to each other. I want to feel love only for you, want to obliterate thought or memory of anyone else but you, whereas you don't want your empire to shrink. May be it is because of something wanting in my love, or your dread of the emptiness you might have to face in the event of my not being there in your life, or plain greed, or whatever. That is why even when you are with me, the moment you get a phone call, you turn off from here and switch on there. Even in very intimate moments with me, you are wrapped in thoughts of somebody else. When you favour somebody, the other feels deprived ... then you run towards him. You are under the illusion that you have a lot to give ... but if it is so, why do I feel deprived? Why does this thought sometimes assail me that all ties between us have snapped? You very often appear to be an image of perplexity. The awareness that I simply increase your tension instead of lessening it adds to my suffering. Thanks to the business of granting favours, you have to manage 'entries' – when one can come, when one cannot ...

I have no authority to tell you that you should limit this empire of yours. According to you, why I or anyone, for that matter, should have this authority at all? But in my case, I do feel good if there be someone whom I may hand over full authority in regard to my life. It may sound romantic, but in our world such a relationship is so rare where you hand over everything of yours to somebody, what a mega asset it is! But today, people are so worldly wise and relations so volatile that you chew them like Paan Bahar and spit out. Mundane existence tinged with a little titillation! Here I am, bound to be misconstrued.

How to say, Suvi, that all this, which is happening is not right! I have put you on a very high pedestal in my life, with you there what depths I fathom, heights I reach … all these will not let me be clever with you. You, too, will perhaps find it difficult to be clever with me, though you are making such an effort now. The upheaval that has come about is like life protesting … to ignore it further will be difficult for you too.

I think the happiness that I got in your company is not my luck anymore. Your rich and full life brimming with thrill and excitement, busier than a bee's – it will more or less sustain you. If you are going to be hurt a little for losing me, you would also feel relieved … but when you again meet some right person, you will have to begin from here only … with these very questions.

When, after making me cool my heels at a certain point, you suddenly blow up your fuse, I feel so lonely, so helpless. Earlier, the pain of such jolts was not so hurtful. But parallel to our growing mutual fondness, these jolts have also become more and more agonizing. The distress through which I have passed during the last few days … I don't think I can take it anymore … so a new beginning, as you also wish, can be made by letting our emotions dry up. We will meet like today … not alone. I continue to visit your place occasionally, just as others do, give you a little tickle, which evaporates with the next gush of wind.

But even if we meet like this, there won't be just the tickle alone, rather we will throw on each other the light of twinkling stars, however faint. And that is the difference.

– Anant

Mansarovar

'Want to be with you … for quite some time,' she said.

'But earlier you had no time to spare.'

'That was then.'

'Shall we be going out?'

'If you so desire, but first come over here.'

Authority stamped with love. I got drawn as I hadn't met her for months. I was the one who was impatient to meet her; my impatience merely found words through her.

In a little while, we were in our favourite haunt. The sun was behind us, in front lush green lawns, and here and there overgrown grass being mowed. On one side, repairs and renovation of a historical building were in progress.

'I have a lot to share with you. All these days, I have been brooding and brooding,' I said.

'Me too. Suddenly, it struck me that I can share everything with you. You alone can appreciate. But first, we'll walk, just walk.'

Ahead was a climb and the way beyond. At the point where the ascent ended, the trees seemed to be stooping, as if bending down with their own weight towards the ground.

'How come you felt that you could share everything with me?' I asked her while walking by her side.

'Maybe a conviction that arose all of a sudden … don't know. I felt our relationship is a sort of prop, constant and stable and will ever remain so. Relations with others are superficial, always in the make-or-break mode.'

I, too, had felt the same.

How is it possible that two persons come to feel the same way at the same time … one feels it and the other voices it? One sitting far away yearns to meet and the other, all of a sudden, comes post haste?

We were strolling without break, sometimes on the gravel lane and sometimes on the pathway in the grass. Somewhere straight, elsewhere circular. As usual, she was intently observing the surroundings and commenting about them, and I, as always, immersed in her. After taking a big round, we sat down on a spot in the grass.

'I think we can now talk about Shyam Mohan also,' I said a little diffidently.

'Yes, why not?' she responded without any compunction.

'Then tell me….'

'Not this way, I can't. You just ask me and I'll answer.'

'Do you love him?'

'What do you mean by love?'

'Oh, now I have to tell you about this too! What I mean … you are impatient to meet him, feel bad if unable to do.'

'No, nothing of the sort. But I do feel good when I meet him. He is a nice person. A gentleman to the core, clean.

Always at hand to help others. He is always in a jovial mood. In his company, you feel light-hearted and vibrant. I'm fond of him….'

Now this language – 'fond of him'. It occurred to me that this common vocabulary was not adequate to express what she feels. Problem arises there.

'Any physical relationship?'

'What type?'

'Of any type.'

'I don't attach importance to all this. The real thing is that rapport where some physicality does creep in.'

'If I'm not wrong, you need everyone. Sometimes you need Shyam Mohan, then me, and sometimes Ramesh.' I couldn't help telling her about her revolving-door affairs.

'Maybe you are right. I feel I am in search of such a person, in whose company I'll be able to live life in all its dimensions. Whoever I have met so far just about fills only a part of me.'

'Will there ever be such a person?'

'Now see … it is a different sort of relationship. I can sit with you and talk for hours. I can't sit with Shyam Mohan too long. After a little while, it seems there is not much left to talk about. Have to scratch your head to find topics to converse, and what we talk about is generally a repeat of what usually takes place with anybody in the office. The way I can feel relaxed with you isn't possible with him. You can just sit with him. Yes … we like each other … and if he gets something from me, why should I stop him?'

'I can't forbid you, nor do I have any right to give any direction to your life. But can you give everything to all?'

'Not to all, but surely to those who I consider my own.'

'Who will you consider your own?'

'Whoever I happen to like.'

'How many can you consider your own at the same time?'

'In my opinion, any good relationship, instead of inhibiting our emotions, makes us liberal. If it prevents us from forming another relationship, it's making us narrow-minded.'

'All of a sudden, you come very close to me, and likewise, with a sudden jerk, you move away. Then distances arise between us. Does the reason for this lie in your living life at different levels with different persons?'

'No, but there must have been something wanting in me that so far I haven't succeeded in generating that feeling in you. My aura remains with you only till I am with you; can linger a little further. But yours remains with me always.'

'Listen, that day you said that you weren't anybody's personal property. But love is a relationship where we, on our own volition, become somebody else's property.'

'Love appeals to me because here we present the best of ourselves. We want to be that which the other person wants us to be. But you do want to be yourself also just as you are … full of pits, wallowing in mud, morose, out of joint. Don't know what is what … nor do I brood over it. I just let things happen. It's owing to you that I have made a small beginning in thinking things over.'

'Is it good or bad?'

'Good. But no good either to be always thinking like you do. What's the use of this thinking that will give only pain as you have been causing to yourself these days. I don't think much, but this much I know that it's you alone with whom I can talk about any matter without hesitation. My other relations come in view only in your light. Our relations rest on a firm basis and will remain so; others will come and go.'

'But they would be more colourful, wouldn't they?' playfully I tried to tease her.

'Maybe, but they won't last long. Firm basis has its own importance.'

'Why do you see me in a different light?'

'My relations with others didn't progress so gradually as with you, neither did they last long … so you are in a league of your own.'

'Rather, it seems to me that your relations with anybody never ever break.'

'Why, relations with Deepak and Som are almost over in a way. Som was a kid. With him, I couldn't ever forget that he is so much younger than me. Deepak was very passionate. This does not go well in life. See his poems. He began to expect that I would give up everything and go to him. Got angry. Now he just continues to write poems. Will send his book without revealing his whereabouts.'

'Deepak's high voltage feelings, Som's young age, Shyam's virtues, I don't possess any of these attributes.'

'No, but you do possess a little of everything. Nowadays, I like to think about you.'

'Just nowadays. That means tomorrow it would be somebody else?'

'Don't such things happen? If they do, why should we talk pompously?'

'Your quest for such a man as will fulfil you in every which way … that superman….'

'Not quest, but desire.'

'Ok … desire, but there's no one like this. It's only our feelings that create such a person. But you never let your feelings come to that stage.'

'Perhaps, I put it wrongly. Desire not for a person but for something that will so fill me that nothing remains wanting thereafter. Even if that fulfilment doesn't come, at least the restlessness would subside.'

'Feelings are the ladder that will help you reach this goal. But you refuse to allow any room for feelings. Without the help of this ladder, you want to jump onto a lofty perch. How is it possible!'

Suvarna seemed to be lost in thought. She would pluck a blade of grass lying nearby, bring it towards herself, and then throw it away.

'I think I rush to explore heights, the peak in every relationship that will light up a dark corner inside me. No denying that I do not find myself fulfilled by any object or person. Since I fail to fulfil myself, I seek vicarious comfort out of watching some others like you fulfilling themselves. This gives some solace … I rush headlong, seeking fulfilment, wander about, and retreat! Either out of fear or boredom, I give up and sit down. With you I find myself secure, because I feel I am at last getting moored somewhere!'

'You must always be finding yourself in a dilemma as to who you like more and who you can leave for whom.'

'No, nothing like that.'

'Who do you love? Can you give a straight answer?'

'Yes, by all means.'

'Who?'

'Ramesh.'

Her reply dumbfounded me. Did I want to hear my name? No, but certainly I hadn't expected either that she would name Ramesh.

'Yes, it's correct. Nobody else is to me what Ramesh is. He takes great care of me. His genial personality extricates me whenever I get tied up in knots.'

'What's the need for getting entangled somewhere else after Ramesh's love?'

'Yes, there is no need. But what am I to do? It happens with me. These, my external relations, I do get so much out of them. They help me in my growth, and that is also something I have to ensure. Love is not the sole thing in the world.'

Silence descended upon us. The sun warming the lawns was receding, so the breeze was spreading chillness around.

'Let's go,' she said after some time.

We got up. The shadows between the big edifices and the trees had lengthened. Darkness was descending on us and there was a nip in the air.

'It is your birthday on the 24th. I'll give you something.'

'Why should you? It's I who will give you.'

'What will you give me?'

'Whatever you ask.'

'Anything I ask!'

'Yes!'

'Think it over! I can ask for anything.'

'Yes, ask for anything. I'll give it to you.'

So large-hearted! I could have run away with her somewhere for a couple of days … could have slept with her … all this could have been mine for the asking. This would have put her in a predicament, though she had made the offer without reservation. But she had full confidence in me that I would never ask for such a thing as could put her in a catch-22 situation.

'So what do you want?' she asked, as I had kept mum.

'Why should I scale down what I want by spelling it out? You must have guessed right. Even if you haven't, you won't be able to give despite your wanting to. It isn't in our hands to give just anything.'

She continued to walk in silence. The ground below was uneven, so she plodded along with unsteady steps, slipping at ascents, landing on sandy patches with a thump, staggering on stone-strewn terrain, feet sinking in wet soft ground.

'How I wish to be with you in the hills? Clasping your hand, race along far and wide. Clear skies, bright sun, air cool and clean.'

There was a glimmer of dream in her eyes. Don't know what reverie made her sway with delight as she walked by my side. I, too, couldn't remain untouched by the warmth of her happy mood.

A little later, on our way back, she looked grave.

'What are you thinking?' I asked her.

'I have been thinking since yesterday that I am getting very close to you. Earlier, it wasn't so.'

'Is it because of disappointment with somebody else?' I teased her.

'Don't be silly. Since I have no expectations anywhere, so no disappointment either. But as for you … sometimes it so happens that you suddenly discover ….'

My hand dropped on her beautiful round arm; I went on stroking it gently. Is this her real self … tinged with little sadness, oozing with emotions, eager to plunge into depths? She is not that person who I had seen some days back in the office … chewing *Paan Bahar* and, with her 'oomph', throwing everyone into the dustbin.

'Sometimes my ardour for you tends to go out of control. I have to restrain myself.'

'Don't restrain. I like it when you touch me.'

'Now I can tell you that you may go to Shyam whenever you want to. It is perhaps owing to my reaching that stage where we are more concerned about our partner's happiness.'

'No, now you are convinced that our relationship won't get sour on account of him. Earlier, you were sensing this danger, so you were distressed, weren't you?'

We were crossing a bridge. Low-hanging bulbs were throwing light on the midway, turning it golden.

'Want to be always with you. How about you?' I asked her.

'We ought to rein in our hearts.'

'What do you think … without you now, I can't….'

'Maybe not.' Her voice sounded cool and collected.

She stopped her car in a dark corner and quietly came in my arms.

'These days our meetings have grown one too many,' she whispered.

'You mean you don't like it?'

'No, no, I didn't mean that ….' saying this, she detached herself and continued.

'If you meet too often, you are out of sorts elsewhere; everything else appears useless. This shouldn't happen – overdependence on a single object. We are nearing the danger mark.'

'Okay, then we should bid adieu.'

'You fool….'

And she laughed … bright sun coming through the clouds, petals of red smooth lips, white pearly teeth.

'Damn.'

'What's the matter?'

'Don't know … I'm fed up.'

'With what … and with whom?'

'With my job … with everything. I don't like to continue with this job.'

'Then get yourself transferred elsewhere. You have so many friends in important positions.'

'I won't ask anyone. I don't like to serve anymore.'

'Then what? Women like you can't live without a job either. Will you be able to lead your life as a housewife and homemaker? A mode of life, apparently fulfilling and important, surrounded by hangers-on, sense of self-importance for holding a prestigious position – we get too habituated to these trappings of office to live without them.'

'Don't know … I don't understand anything. I'm restless, that's about it. Sometimes I think of opening a dancing school.'

'So many times you started dancing and gave it up. The feeling of ennui does overtake us when we only think of filling our emptiness. Life's essence can be savoured by plumbing the depths, while there you just tread on the surface. However, this dancing school, that isn't a bad idea; you have been fond of dancing. What happened to your plan of doing post-graduation in dancing? You had filled the form, hadn't you?'

'Yes, I had. But I can't do all this now … going through the grind of preparing for an examination and the like. What's the use of going for another master's degree? I'm simply bored stiff.'

All of a sudden, leaving me behind, she ran on the path in front. She must have sprinted a hundred yards. Reaching across there, she was filling her lungs with quick breaths and looking at me. Then she sat down and waited for me.

On my approaching her, she got up. We resumed our walking.

'Tell me, do you ever think about my body?' she asked me as if this thought had been agitating her for quite some time.

'Why? I do think quite a deal. Often I feel that every part of your body must be very sweet, have a strong desire to plant kisses on you from every side.'

'Then?' Her eyes lit up.

'I find myself in a dilemma that this might be nothing but carnal appetite. I hail from a town where even touching a girl is a big boon; takes years to reach that point. Female body is an object of great attraction for me, so I am extra cautious; if your sole interest is in the body, other things take a back seat … just as they slip away from a person who is obsessed with money. The real beauty lies within … manifests itself gradually but lasts very long.'

'You mean to say that the body has no significance whatsoever?'

'No, it's very significant, but in tandem with love. I'm amazed to know that people don't love each other and yet can enjoy sex.'

Seemingly, in part bafflement and part reminiscent mood, she continued to walk. She would kick away small stones and pebbles with her sandals.

'When I'm not in the mood for it, I keep Ramesh away. Both should be on the same wavelength. Our sex life is good;

feel nice generally as after a delectable meal, but sometimes as if we've drifted away from each other. This taboo on extra marital relations … it's sheer nonsense.'

Today, not only her job but all other ties were galling her, while she wanted so much to flow on unhindered. She was walking with her hands in the trouser pockets, inhaling the air with every breath.

'I often dream of passing one full night with you where the body and the soul weld together into singleness. How singular, life-giving this experience will be…!'

This erotic outpouring on my part resulted in my fantasizing that in the night's darkness, like a bunch of bright moonlight, she was lying covered with only a thin transparent sheet, a delicious languor stealing over her sensuous body, a mellow fragrance of sandalwood emanating from it. My eyes and lips picked her up to carry her into infinity.

She heard every word of mine, spellbound. We were standing near a tree, lost in each other.

'Can't you give me one night out of your life's numerous ones?'

She was startled. She shook herself into consciousness at my propositioning, and started walking.

'We are okay as we are. Come on … let's race together.'

Saying this, she clasped my hand and, almost dragging me, ran forward. Running, we crossed the mound in front.

On reaching the top, we stood facing each other, trying to get our breath back. Then we sat down on a greenish bench, half-hidden under a dense bougainvillea bush.

'Time to have a crush ... life has become too boring,' she said.

'What's this crush?'

'Don't know crush? Well, well! Chance meeting and vibing with somebody, revelling and frolicking, visiting pubs and hotels, and also spiced up with some romance. After these escapades, the prodigal returns home....'

'This is what you are already doing.'

'What am I doing?'

'What I mean is that, leaving out the sex aspect, everything else in your wish list is already taking place ... not only with me but with others too.'

'Don't be silly ... a crush doesn't last so long.'

Occasionally, it seems that in her mind there is a format as per which she wants to live ... with any man that suits her fancy. This is the crux of her restlessness. With her there, I can't think of any other relationship. I get everything in it and can remain immersed in it for days together ... and contrarily, here is she who loves her husband, is intimate with a couple of others, even then she is hankering after a crush.

Do these words – affair, crush – go down well with us? A chance encounter with somebody, striking up a romantic relationship and then retreating from it without compunction – this is the template of modernity.

'Will you call what's between us an affair?'

'No.'

'Then what's it?'

'No clue ... but don't you abandon me. I'm a naughty girl, always be around me.'

Her eyes were on the verge of getting moist. I placed my hand on hers and pressed it in a sort of reassuring gesture. A chirpy, vivacious girl, given to some flirting, forming relationships somewhat uninhibitedly; maybe this suited her to a tee. And there lies the rub. Even all these could not fulfil her totally. Her chirpiness on display was a mere facade; deep within she was sad, regardless of whether she accepted it or not.

'You did have many admirers, but you never got love in the true sense ... nobody could reach you.'

'You seem to be right. We can't also run away from the fact that restlessness in this middle age of ours is rather on the high side. In our youth, we have a couldn't-care-less attitude – your whole life lies stretched before you; it appears if not today there's always a tomorrow. But on reaching our age, we start feeling desperate.'

'It's not a matter of any specific period or age. Everyone needs love at every stage of life. To me, it appears that this is the very thing that keeps a person alive and, as for me, I need oodles of love.'

'That's why you can give it to others. Isn't it strange that the more a person is thirsty, the more he is able to quench the thirst of another person? I had told Shyam once that my relation with Anant is what I used to dream about.'

Her fine eyebrows were rising and falling gently like small fish frisking in the water. Her face resembled a bud burgeoning into a blossom. As emotions surfaced one after the other, her face would light up.

'I'm gravitating towards you rather fast,' she added. 'It scares me – what am I going to do on reaching the point where I would be wanting to be with you, all the time, to live with you?'

'I've already reached that stage. I've been living with this longing since long.'

'I'm not used to living in destitution. I fear lest I do what both of us don't want to. So far, we haven't deviated from our resolve that we'd stick to our limits.'

Fear of being uprooted from the frame! She had everything and she was quite happy with it too. I'd awakened the dormant sadness within her. She has begun to feel that on the face of it, everything is hunky-dory, but…! Maybe I haven't acted right, so should I have let her live under illusions?

She kept looking at me, quiet and sad. Her eyes betrayed the intense inner turmoil. Gradually, her head lolled against my shoulder. Silence swept over us, not even the sound of breathing disturbing it. Next moment, two big tears fell on my shirt.

Once she'd told me that crying didn't come to her easily. Once in a long while, if at all, she gives in to crying, that too briefly and in solitude, concealed from Ramesh. I, too, saw her in this crying mode for the first time.

'No harm crying like this sometimes,' I patted her. Leaving aside one's ego and sapience, how light one feels by handing over everything to someone and thus deflating oneself.

A tiny pigeon lying inert in my lap ... fluttering, perplexed for being over-wise. She was looking to me for guidance. How could I guide her when I myself hadn't understood her fully.

She remained in that position for some moments. When she saw someone coming from the opposite side, she separated herself from me and wiped her eyes. Getting up from the bench, she lay down on the grass nearby.

'When I get tired of too much thinking, I give it up and start chanting the Gayatri Mantra.'

'Well, well! Do you worship?'

'Yes, daily. You do not believe, do you?'

'No, not that. I just couldn't associate it with you.'

She looked up at me in surprise, then her eyes began to roam across the expanse of the sky. Framed against the clear blue sky could be seen a bird hung in the air.

'Look there ....' Her face lit up. 'How easily birds float in the sky! Why can't we do the same?'

'Only those who can fly can float in the air.'

She didn't pay heed; was lost in the bird swinging above, attuned to its flight, and far far away from me!

12 January 1979

How far have I come ... from where to where.

How a being, its every fibre melting, flows into another! I can directly feel the delight of this flowing. I've arrived up to this point, for sure.

I have become more dependent on her … this is making her cautious. She is worried that we may now have to face things untoward. Once she had also said that she didn't like any pain-causing relationship. Maybe, this is the reason that she wants to maintain a balance with a view to 'managing' things. She's apprehensive that a situation may arise when we are compelled to lose each other. Who knows, behind these fears lies her real fear of losing her balance? Her worry as to what will happen to me in that situation is actually her concern about losing her balance.

How very stupid of us! Life lies before us with an open bag of gifts – take your pick – and here we are standing in dread of scorching our fingers. We do need fire, but can't sit too close to it. For experiencing the fire of love, we need a fire within ourselves – the fire of youth, abandon, or ignorance. The fear of this fire engulfing her home torments her. These roost-like homes that we inherit don't assuredly keep us happy, but neither can we live without them. We chase novel experiences, but can't digest the distance that we have covered in this pursuit. She feels that we have rather come too far. Scared, she makes hasty retreats time and again. The result is akin to the antics of the toy-monkey, which goes up at one leap and the next moment falls back landing on its original spot.

She only gives … rarely ever is she seen taking. She's incapable of asking for anything. Just as not everyone is gifted with the capacity to love, so she too lacks it. In love, you have also to ask for as much as to give.

I almost hit the bull's eye in my logical and psychological analysis of her behaviour and, more or less, of her total persona, yet she is not that person who descends in my inner self step by step emotionally. These two images of hers fall apart, and then it appears to me that either she is lost somewhere in that logical analysis or is sandwiched somewhere in this guessing game ... that which she really is.

These days, I remain immersed in deep but sweet depths for hours. As if her beauty has melted and spread all over in the atmosphere. It is in the air and I inhale it in every breath. I find myself enveloped with affinity like moonlight raining from the sky. Fragrance ... of being constantly under the shadow of her beautiful neck.

All these are more beautiful than she is. I have to take pains to remember her features. But she is with me always. Maybe this is what love is ... when the quintessence of the loved one reaches you, leaving the physical far behind. Now, even a gentle physical contact with her overwhelms me with her quintessence.

How beautiful life is! Sweetness all around. That yellowing circle around the crescent moon, raining coolness, this girl's beauty probably originates from there.

Look, Mian Tansen's Haveli!

Suvarna had mentioned once, just as she did about her friends, only when called upon, in measured words, conveying minimal information in such a way that the relations between that man and Suvarna may appear absolutely commonplace. The other day when I reached her office, they were talking on the phone. I couldn't help asking her after she had finished. It was Arvind, she told; he works here only, rings up sometimes or drops in.

I wonder if she mentions my name to others in a similar manner? After the Shyam Mohan episode, I'd begun to take her statements with a pinch of salt. Where she happens to be praising a person in glowing terms, you can take it that her relations with him are formal. When she speaks guardedly about a person, downgrading her relationship with him, there's bound to be more than meets the eye.

She'd come to the office after a brief sickness. I was eager to enquire about her health. So I went to her office without informing her beforehand. He was with her in her room at that time.

Arvind was sitting in a corner on an armchair – fair complexion, broad face, big eyes. If you ignore the slightly thick lips, he could be considered handsome. He was somewhere between thirty-five and forty. The time was the same when we usually met – a little before the office-closing hour, which could be stretched to anything from sitting in the quiet solitude of the room to leaving the office for an outing.

'This is Arvind....' she introduced us. 'And this is Anant ... told you.' Last two words, almost whispered, betrayed the intimacy between the two.

'No tea or coffee, canteen is closed,' she expressed her helplessness in the beginning itself.

'Don't bother,' I said, 'water will do. How long have you been here, Mr Arvind?'

'Three years.'

'You had recently been abroad?'

'Yes.'

'She had told me. When did you return?'

'A week ago.'

'Must have brought a lot of goodies?'

'Not much actually.'

'Had taken your family?'

'No, they were here.'

'How many children?'

'Two.'

'No water either,' Suvarna came in, upending the empty thermos.

'Do you propose to go abroad again on deputation?'

'Don't think any such proposal is in the pipeline.'

'Then you'll remain in this very department?'

'Looks like.'

'How long is your present tenure for?'

'Five.'

'Deputation abroad must be easily resulting in a windfall … lakhs.'

'Maybe so.'

'Then why don't you try to go abroad again?'

Arvind kept silent. I was relentlessly posing question after question … wasn't sure if I'll get a chance of meeting him again. I thought I should know a little about someone who was so close to Suvarna. She, on her part, was fidgeting in her chair.

'She speaks very highly of you,' I said further.

Arvind managed to force a laugh. It tickled me to think that he must have felt hurt to learn that Suvarna talked about him to me. Suvarna's lips were sealed, fearing God knows what I might further ask, maybe something very embarrassing. The formal smile that had come on her face when I arrived had completely disappeared. Arvind's face wore a blank look. He appeared to be a reserved and practical type … a cold sort of person.

'My apologies. I was passing this way, thought I'd enquire about your health….' I made an attempt to be courteous. 'I'll take your leave.'

'Yes, time to leave. It's already fifteen minutes past the close of office….' Suvarna seemed relieved. She began to collect her things. Arvind kept sitting in silence, as if anticipating that she would manage to get rid of me and they would be able to sit together for some more time.

'So not even water, have to go back thirsty.' I got up.

That moment, she must have certainly disapproved of my choice of words, but she continued to give the impression that I was only alluding to water and there was no need to read too much into what I had said. After shaking hands with Arvind, I came out. While I was coming out, she didn't forget to say 'bye' to me.

There is certainly a demon inside human. When it wakes up, we become oblivious to what we are doing or saying. Outside her office, I continued to walk about mechanically, as if it was imperative for me to meet Suvarna here and now, or to know how long they sit together alone in office. This tiresome waiting was aggravating my already foul temper. At long last, exhausted by this waiting, again I retraced my steps towards her room, expecting that Arvind might have left by now and she might still be there. She met me on the stairs, alone. I returned with her. We didn't exchange a word, as there were people around coming in and going out. After coming out, she put on her goggles and headed for the car park with me in tow.

'Was keen to meet you today, after your bout of illness. How are you?'

'I'm all right,' her voice sounded standoffish.

She kept walking silently. On reaching the car, she quietly unlocked it, but before getting in she paused a little and faced me.

'What was the need for those searching questions? Were you out to humiliate me?'

'No, no! How could I ever think of such a thing? I'd met him for the first time, so was curious to know about him.'

'You could've asked me.'

I remembered when I was bombarding questions at him, there was a look of apprehension in her eyes … the same which appears in the eyes of a pigeon protecting its eggs.

'You could have told him about me….'

'Of course he knows about you.'

'Only that much which is necessary for your game.'

'For God's sake, don't quarrel here on the road.'

'Suvi, why do you need to wander here and there? You better control this before it turns into a disease.'

She had the least interest in my advice. She just kept mum, got into the car, and drove away, ignoring me completely.

Like a drunken man reviewing his shenanigans of a previous inebriated condition, I was feeling guilty and, in equal measure, surprised at what had happened. Where was this side of mine hidden all this while?

Had the matter stopped there, the hurt would not have been so deep. She, too, had been trying to restrain me from unrelentingly asking such trivial and insinuating questions. The following days there was no call from her side. When I rang up, she disconnected after a brief and formal response. When I proposed to meet her, she blandly informed me that she would be busy with official work for some days. On several occasions, I'd myself used this ploy to evade people seeking appointment with me, so I didn't give up.

'Look here!' I said on the phone on my third try. 'I'm very upset. After meeting you only will I feel relieved. Our relations are so precious. Is it proper to let them break merely due to some misunderstanding? All right, a little dishonesty had crept in. Should we not think of throwing it out? I'll come over whenever you are free.'

She listened for some time and then, asking me to come at 4:30, hung up sort of dismissively, otherwise I'd have gone on talking. She didn't like to discuss such matters on phone.

I reached there right on the dot. She was alone in the room. A cold reception awaited me. 'Come, be seated.' No 'hi', nor a welcome smile. She wore a serious look and, in a silent mode, remained immersed in files. After finishing one, she would pick up another. In the meantime, she rang up the canteen for two teas. I was wondering how long I'd be sitting like this. If she's really busy, why am I needlessly imposing myself on her … why can't I be similarly busy to avoid her?

The bearer came and placed the tea tray. She raised her head from the file to pay him. Then again, she busied herself in a file. Biting the pen with her lips, she perused the file, then wrote a note of a few lines and put the file in the out tray. Thereafter, she pulled the tea tray to her side and started making the tea.

'Yes, now tell me….' she said, like officers do to persons visiting them.

After stirring the tea, she placed the cup before me. Now she was facing me fully and looking straight into my eyes. I was wondering where to start and on what topic. Of course, it was just a pretext to be with her. Earlier too, I had felt a number of times whether it was really worthwhile appraising time and again what was going on between the two of us and accordingly draw varying inferences from it. Isn't it just good enough that we are there together? Our trysts constitute real happiness; why not let ourselves be immersed in them? This is what she tries to do; it's I who makes a fetish of dragging her into introspecting over and over.

'So sorry for that day. Don't know what came over me.'

She said nothing.

'How are you feeling now?'

'Here I am, sitting before you. Drink your tea.'

'Why are you speaking in such a matter-of-fact way?'

'I can't always speak the way you want me to. And why at all should I? I too can wish to have my way, or has it always to be yours?'

'Individual ways are always there; they become mutual when we begin to care more about the other.'

'I have to take care of myself too. If I were to always worry about others, I'd find myself reduced to a zombie. I have also to protect myself.'

'This too doesn't make any difference if there's basic understanding between us … and the trust that we belong. This trust gets firmer if we keep sharing with each other and confiding as well.'

'Confiding what?'

'Everything....'

'That's just bullshit. Can any person reveal everything to another?'

'One can … at least broadly.'

'No. I can't do that. I'm a private sort of person. And why should I … why? I have dozens of friends. You men have only this attitude of viewing every man–woman relationship as a clandestine affair. It's expected of me that I keep clearing your narrow-mindedness, give details of all my relationships. Why, but why should I do all this? Let anyone think whatever he or she wants to … huh!'

'….'

'Look here, Anant,' her eyes blazed with fury. 'If you think that I should tell you whatever I do, do things after reflecting what you like or dislike, then I won't be able to do so. I have my own likes and dislikes, my own individuality. It's absurd that every time I have to give an explanation … like I have to take a test and pass it. Every time I have to vouch before you that I feel as intensely for you as you do for me. If it isn't like weighing on a scale, then what's it? My foot!'

Suppressed anger had burst open. Her eyebrows went up and down of their accord, as they also did when she had softer feelings inside. How strange!

'If you feel,' she went on, 'that I surely do not give you what you give me or you don't get your wish or I am not what you desire me to be, then okay, we end it here and now. I have not kept you bound.'

'Is it so easy?'

'If not for you, that's your problem. Would I keep taking the test lifelong?'

'The issue is not of test but of fortifying the trust that is between us, of strengthening it.'

'I can't do all that. I am what I am. And why should I do it, just because you like it or want it? I may also have my likes and dislikes.'

'In love, we also do what would keep us exalted in the eyes of our beloved. Doing something just for our partner's sake can by itself be a matter of great joy.'

'This isn't love but suicide, to hurt oneself for another's sake. Love is that which opens us, not one to close us down … drives away our tedium, fills us with zing and zest. A relationship that fails to achieve this is useless, call it love or whatever.'

She was looking at me as though she was as much irked with me as with my heavy-duty words.

'This other one … does he count for nothing in your scheme of things?' I couldn't help asking.

'I don't know.' Her words were spiked with annoyance, maybe as much with my uncomfortable questions as with my habit of directing a barrage of questions.

'Will you never want to do something for this other one?'

'No, never at my cost!'

'If this other one happens to be a person who you are also fond of a little bit … even then not?'

'I can't do all this. It's too much of a strain for me. I'm all right as I am. Will I go on trying to elevate myself all my life because someone likes this? No, thank you! Instead of wasting my time there, why shouldn't I lead my life on my own terms and to my heart's content? It's my life and I want to live it my way. Anant, I don't want you to remain under any illusion. If you have any reservations to this approach of mine, then goodbye!'

What we had created piecing together bits and fixing layer upon layer of emotions was collapsing in a jiffy. And there I was, watching it like the child who sees his sandcastle crumbling, caving in and being swept away in the torrential rain.

'You called it dishonesty. Pray, what dishonesty I'm guilty of and with whom? You are seeking an explanation from me as if you were my husband. What vows have I exchanged with you ... tell me?'

Just as a punching bag receives a shower of blows from a boxer, I was getting hit right and left, up and down. When, for the first time, my head had unconsciously rested on her neck, why hadn't she shrugged me off there and then? Conjointly, we had then touched borders of godhood.

Those heights ... depths ... they had to come to such a pass! If, at the end of the day, this is what destiny holds for us, why do we set out to build nests?

Her contentions sulphurous, menacing tone ... and my answer to them; tears coming out in a stream ... further presenting me as a weakling. As for her, she never sheds tears, because in her book one shouldn't exhibit one's weakness before others but always put on a brave face.

'That day I just sat silent. Sometimes I was looking at you, sometimes at Arvind, as though I was some inanimate object lying between you two. I shouldn't keep you under any delusion. I'll have to give it serious thought, probe thoroughly within whether I still feel the same way for you as before....' her brutal onslaught continued.

To hear from her in a couple of words that she was fed up with me required a lot of courage for me, which, for sure, I didn't possess at all. Sparing me that torture, she conveyed it alright.

There was a method in her roundabout way, which was primarily meant to convey to me ... go away please ... leave me alone now ... enough is enough. It would have been better if this decision had been taken by both of us together. Then the parting of ways would have been graceful and without rancour. Graciousness in dealing has always been her credo too, but in life things don't always pan out the way we want them to.

8 May 1979

Totally bewildered ... that which has happened ... has it really happened? How could she, who I have almost adored, think that I am humiliating her? How could I have caused such anguish to her, who I've never ever thought of hurting even slightly. I, too, have been in extreme torment for the last few days, have been the target of severe rebuke ... and thank you for it. Believe me, I never felt bad at your stinging words ... there is a personal touch when you rebuke somebody, which is why we can't rebuke just anyone. Now I want somebody to wipe our hearts clean of this clutter of unpleasant things ... but who will it be? What made me utter the word 'dishonesty'? It was a wrong word, though viewed in the context of my love, it wasn't that wrong either. To me, our relationship has always been a bond of love ... if I were to view everything from that standpoint, no wrong was committed (no question of right and wrong, I will view that way only). I may complain that when this very standpoint prompts me to think of sweet and beautiful things about you, you relish it, but if it turns out to be something that doesn't suit you, limits your freedom, you condemn it outright. Why do we always want to get only good things from a person? An individual will give only in accordance with what he is, as we have accepted him. By the same token, I too shouldn't be put off by something of yours just because it doesn't suit me, because you are what you are.

Your reluctance to give our relationship a name was more appropriate than your insistence on calling it a friendship with the epithet 'very dear'! What passed between us, the give-and-take, what we felt for each other right from the beginning, can we do all that with every Tom, Dick, and Harry? Even in the West, a girl just offers her cheek to acquaintances; she grants special favours only to the person she loves. Having come as far as we have, can our relationship be viewed as mere friendship? Doesn't trust in love have to be manifested at every step? Perhaps, this is the difference between conjugal relationship and this relationship where there is a perpetual demand for manifesting trust; it's not for nothing that lovers repeatedly whisper to each other, 'I love you'... same spontaneous expression in intense moments of intimacy. You might say we aren't lovers. Okay, even if you are not while I am, will this demand still be unforgivable? No denying I overdo things at times. Maybe for the past few days, I've been somewhat more impatient, greedy too, not so much for the physical as for savouring the emotional that I had missed all these months.

When there is too much concern to have a firm grip on life, very often it slips away. And that is what happened to me. In the days ahead, I won't be able to forgive myself, even if she forgives me. For sure she will forgive me, because as a person she is much, much taller than I am. Maybe this is my problem – I'm simply deep but lack broad-mindedness. Where will I find it? In which pit should I fling my pettiness? You have tolerated it a lot. Can you give me stature? Maybe not now, for you show me the door, every time: 'If not like this, okay, let us call it a day.' There, yonder, you see the haveli of Mian Tansen! 'For God's sake, leave me alone.' This is for the second time that I've been shown the door. Next time, sonny, you will be most unceremoniously kicked out. Everyone wants happiness. How long will anybody tolerate you wearing a long face? Why should anyone take pains to look within you? So whatever needs to be done now, has to be done by you alone, with yourself.

That said, a positive thing has also emerged from this incident. Though you never spelt out in so many words, you did mean to say that in needless analysis, why we squander moments given to us to live them in full. Whether it is friendship or love … so what? Each of them is precious, buddy. My bad luck, she is no longer there to say, 'Look, what bird is it!'

I concede it's difficult to get along with me because I'm quite a complicated person, besides being a big bore. Here I must give you full credit for putting up with a person like me. Must be feeling tired now. I'll do something, but what … don't know as yet.

But no way can I do two things. She who entered my life as someone special right from the very beginning, whose image has ever remained the same … now to consider and deal with her as a casual friend … once I'd thought of doing so, but couldn't. Now never ever would I like to do it. She will ever remain the same, regardless of her consent or not. She's welcome to harbour the notion that I'm no different from others. But for me, she is the only one, she alone.

Secondly, my agony – whether caused due to self-love or infatuation for someone – however unbearable, is a precious thing of life because from it flows our understanding of life, our wisdom, and morality. I don't want to be an ever-jovial dolt. If my appearance remains ominous, then so be it; she may love me or not. This doesn't, however, mean that never ever let your hair down. Can adopt an open and a tad carefree attitude about everything, even while pangs of alienation are dripping from the heart like droplets from a block of ice.

I am not alone. God! You are there. By wiping out the concept of God, some people tried to destroy the higher world and now they are bent upon destroying the earthly world too by eliminating love. Emotions are considered a burden. People fight shy of love, regardless of living their entire lives without giving love or getting love ... all the time feeling complacent for having avoided emotional entanglement and complications. Why does every educated person look sickly to me? Will, at the end of the day, something of this emotive trait survive only in those who haven't been brainwashed by education and the so-called civilization? And my educated friends tell me – it's me who is sick, not they.

Has it become a letter or a diary?

Rebirth

5 June 1979

I am kind of enveloped in the cobweb of sadness; for hours, for days together I am sad.

When a companionship, which made such an impact on my life and personality, leaves behind only sadness, suffice it to conclude that there is nothing but suffering in life. In some company, or owing to some incident or during a period of time, suffering may temporarily abate but only to reignite. Instead of trying to cover this suffering with some external object or company, I should learn to live with it. So I've decided that I'll not run away from my sorrow and desolation; instead I should write my diary profusely. Through diary, one can be one's own companion every moment, everyday. I can consider my diary as my friend.

In the past few days, my relationship with Suvarna had reached a tipping point – me asserting my right over her and she perceiving it as burdensome and tedious, resulting in bitterness in both of us. Thus, this seemingly abrupt rift in our relations was very much on the cards. Is it that there was no solid foundation of our relationship, and all this while we were living in a world of make-believe?

It is not just sorrow caused by separation. It's there alright, but beyond it, the question arises as to whether affinity is of no consequence whatsoever. How can it be possible that of the two, having been so emotionally involved all this while, one has to prod and probe to find out if really he/she had any genuine feelings for the other. If it was ennui caused by a long-drawn association or too much familiarity, then why wasn't I simultaneously affected by it? Not unlikely that I might be having some ingrained shortcoming in me that I cannot keep somebody attached to me for long, or that life as such is governed by the inexorable principle that here all are floating in the flux of time and no one can stay put at one haven for long. We are cursed to remain adrift. How strange that, despite pouring the best of you into somebody, all of a sudden everything goes bust!

Separation from one you have been meeting, talking daily almost … separation in such a manner that you can't even hear her voice! How lonely life has become! I'll have to get used to this.

6 July 1979

Almost the whole night I couldn't get a wink of sleep, was tossing and turning in bed throughout. There was a time when such restlessness of mine would reach her somehow and she would speak soothingly to me about it the very next day. Now...? Even now I think sweetly about her, but the desire to meet her has cooled off. When I think of striking a lone path after separating from her, my mind accepts it but my heart sinks.

The flaw lies somewhere in my life's verve, which probably jumped a little too high.

We initially want a little space, gradually go on acquiring more and more of it; then all of a sudden reach a point where nothing further can be acquired, while the desire still remains the same – to grab the other totally. This is the problem ... the feeling of give-and-take begins to get extinguished there.

Now our helplessness is not that we can't give anything to each other, but that our desire to do so is getting snuffed out. This is a bigger torment. It's like the source of a waterfall going dry.

11 July 1979

Perhaps, I have arrived at that phase of life when people begin to desert you, thus forcing you to fend for yourself, no external support. It appears I am losing the trait which helped me in getting along easily anywhere. These days, for no earthly reason whatever, differences crop up between me and others. Often, I find myself thinking that I can maintain cordial relations with people so long as I keep myself away and aloof from them ... withdrawn into myself. I wonder if some tough stuff is being born inside me that will cut me off from my close friends and social contacts. I will be confined only to those with whom I have just formal relations. What it boils down to is that the will and zest to live, my life's purpose, all this I'll have to seek within myself.

How the pangs of break-up with someone intimate come to you as the torment of breakdown of your own self! If this is the end, why don't we seek solace just in keeping to ourselves? Why run outwards?

Unfortunately, I don't know myself what I have to achieve for which I should strive to become self-dependent .... What can be salvaged where there is nothing but rotting layer after layer of disintegration, frustration, and suffering.

Then comes the feeling that something positive will emerge from this distress – this very trauma. How can this incident, which has devastated so much within, go totally waste?

12 July 1979

It rained in the evening, The weather became pleasant. The feel of cool air on the face lightened the heart, rekindling the desire to meet Suvarna. But the very next moment, I was assailed by doubts – how can I now meet her just by the way without fixing a proper appointment? The moment I enter her room, I may have to face her interrogatory stare. Will she be able to stand even my presence? And heaviness overtook me the same way as I had felt light only moments before. I sank into gloom just like a pitcher after being buffeted by the waves sinks to the bottom.

In view of the fact that we are drying up emotionally so fast, it is unlikely that anything nostalgically worthwhile will remain. As if nothing had happened between the two of us, and we were just nodding acquaintances. Can such a page of life be torn off so easily and thrown away?

Nature … away from the maddening crowd, from associations and tensions … nature … a universe in itself. Why don't I immerse myself in it?

She used to say … do such relations ever die? Is there anything left even now?

15 July 1979

The narrative of life should begin with the mention of death. Where the end is already predestined, every act is transient and every objective set for oneself an illusion. If you want to live without nurturing any illusion, consider your life a brief journey. If, during the journey, this conviction (not merely information) may dawn that sooner or later, everyone has to get down somewhere or the other, then what is left to do while we are up and about is that we share the suffering of others, solve their hurts with love, and treat our co-travellers with compassion, empathy, and affection. Our highest achievement is worthless if it doesn't give impetus to these values. The roadblock to this noble aim is egoism. This egoism can be countered in two ways – we align ourselves so completely with someone that we forget our being or undergo such agony, which makes our existence appear a mere cipher.

Love has both. It is agony; one gets humanized only in the crucible of suffering.

18 July 1979

Could hardly pull on for two months. It was certain that she would never ring up on her own. For her to take the initiative to phone in such a situation meant a definite comedown; she wants always to have the upper hand, as though it isn't love but war. I, on the other hand, thought that a beautiful relationship with a person who has given so much can't be sacrificed merely over a trivial misunderstanding, or our stubbornness and egotist attitude. So I phoned her.

She was caught unawares. Over the phone, I could feel her unease … arising from her and reverting to her.

'You are also feeling bad?' I asked her.

'Yes.'

'Would you like to meet?'

'Yes.'

It was difficult to gauge what these two 'ayes' were soaked in. Uttering this lone word, she was trembling like a leaf quivering in the rain.

'When?'

'Whenever you want to,' this time she had given me the option.

When face-to-face, we stood looking embarrassingly at each other for a short while.

'I am sorry,' she said.

'I suffered the same pain I had given you.'

Don't remember what we talked about; we didn't talk much. Whatever we talked about was mostly formal. We exercised caution. I handed over the diary-like letter that I had penned after that day's face-off. She put it in the drawer for reading it later. I got up as soon as I finished the tea.

'Trust me....' she said gently and stretched her beautiful palm towards me. I let it fall in my hand and held it for sometime. Then suddenly, it struck me that this fair palm must be stretching like this towards some other person or towards anyone for that matter; just a habit, mannerism! Her reassurance seemed to have a hollow ring, devoid of emotion as it were; it sounded meaningless. Maybe this is what they call a wedge between two human beings.

After a long time, it had so happened that I wanted to leave her so early. Though there was temptation on either side that a beginning could be made for a thing that was there before. But there was also a third entity beside us. Time. That time when the mutual give-and-take that happens is cherished for years – that time which is so short in life.

My suffering hasn't cleansed me completely, else I'd have seen in Suvarna an individual who has gone astray but one who is also hurt, like me. Even though not having full faith in love, rather being slightly incapable of it, she's taught me that love does not mean asserting your authority on somebody, or transforming him or her as your clone-love. It is giving yourself completely to your loved one. Despite having different temperaments and traversing our separate paths, we sustain the feeling of being fellow travellers ... thus age together. Conscious that no way can we bear another person's cross, yet we can give the feeling of being near despite being afar.

Will I be able to achieve this?

1 August 1979

From hearsay, I know I was born on this day. I see no grand plan of the Almighty in my coming into this world. There are innumerable people like me. She rang up and insisted on my coming over, even for a short while. A novel, balanced, but subdued excitement was there between us. She put a piece of chocolate in my mouth. As if the touch of her gentle fingers on my lips again came forward to play the melody of life. At length, scratches mingle with the pensive shades of eyes and settle down there, which is why we were looking for them in each other's eyes to give them the soothing touch of love.

We had got back our language of love. An assurance also lurked behind – that since we had managed to retrieve it just when we were about to lose it, we wouldn't now forget it. Neither of us was saying anything; there was no need. The need to speak arises while piecing together such a language or when we don't have this language at all.

Sitting before me in a huddle, she was doodling on a sheet of paper. From time to time, her face would go ruddy … some emotion pricking or the consciousness that we two were close again.

She was lost in thoughts, scribbling or drawing something on paper … me nearby watching her. That moment I felt that the suffering of the past few days had washed out all the dirt that had come to settle on us. We are not simply what we appear outside. Our inner selves had turned out cleaner. Though mere dots on earth, yet a particle of the infinite is there within us. External influences won't succeed in dimming our vision now. My connect with Suvarna's cleaner self will always be there. Love, glowing within, which I was feeling for her then was never so before. The radiance of her innermost self was filling my soul with light.

My eyes shut involuntarily … let the light get brighter.

Florist's Festival

Shyam's birthday.

He should be happy this day. Suvarna keeps herself happy on her birthday, chirping every moment. On some pretext or the other, she will let not only her friends but even acquaintances know beforehand about her coming birthday. That day, the moment she wakes up, she is flooded with greetings from Ramesh and the children with floral bouquets, or with gifts purchased earlier. The phone starts ringing right from the morning, greetings pouring from the city and outside. On entering the office room, she will find a bouquet of fresh flowers adorning the table. Beautiful start to the day! She knows who would have come before her and placed the bouquet. It warms the cockles of her heart to see that she has such friends, so very imaginative. Shyam would follow it up with his call. After greetings, the secret of the presence of flowers in the room will be let out gradually. Though Suvarna already knows that it's Shyam who has brought the flowers, the gradual unfolding of the secret makes the flowers lovelier still. Then Shyam will come and they will have coffee together. In the midst of all this, there's no end of phone calls, a host of visitors showering felicitations. All this exults her and the shower of petals of good wishes is continuous. This day she doesn't want any shadow of sadness to fall on her.

On his birthday, Shyam wanted to spend more time with her. Suvarna was in a predicament. She had to go for a week's training. She wouldn't be in her room. So it was planned that Shyam would come to the training institute at 1 pm, and they will be together during the lunch hour.

Shyam came on time. Suvarna had brought some sweets for him. There was a small park close by, where there were benches under large trees. This was no time to sit there, but then there was no choice. Had they gone elsewhere, the available time would have been taken up in commuting to and fro. They strode towards the park, Shyam sometimes walking by her side, sometimes behind her chatting, and Suvarna would round it off with her laughter. No bickering or argument today, only joy and merriment like gentle ripples of water flowing smoothly and buoyantly over stones and pebbles.

The institute was left behind. The after-rain sun was harsh and the atmosphere heavy with humidity. The purring of cars plying on the road and the occasional rumble of buses passing by … a bird, calling out in a shrill note, flew from one tree to another.

They sat down on a bench under the shade of a tree in the park. Scarcely had Suvarna taken out a piece of sweet from the carton and stretched out her hand towards Shyam's mouth when, God knows from where, Ramesh appeared all of a sudden. No knowing when his car came, where it came from … it was parked in front of the gate through which Suvarna and Shyam had entered minutes before. Ramesh walked towards them with a soldier's gait. Without uttering a word, he grabbed Suvarna's wrist and began to drag her towards the car. The sweet stuck between her fingers crumbled, the pieces scattering on the ground.

'Get into the car,' Ramesh ordered.

Ramesh's face was stiff, his voice harsh and menacing. He didn't even bother to say hello to Shyam. Suvarna couldn't comprehend what she was seeing, or what was happening. Right then, she sighted the driver gazing intently in her direction … Ramesh's driver, who she is used to ordering about. She forced free her hand from Ramesh's tight grip and, without saying a word, proceeded towards the car and got in. Ramesh followed her, opened the door from the other side, and sat beside her. The car started.

Suvarna looked back at the park left behind. There was Shyam standing alone, and on the bench a black smudge that happened to be the carton of sweets. What a denouement! Today was his birthday!

She didn't say anything on the way. When Ramesh tried to speak, she silenced him with a stern look – nothing before the driver. The moment she reached home, she made a beeline for her room, followed by Ramesh. Closing the door, she flew into a rage.

'What the hell do you mean by this insolence, this arrogance? Am I some animal to be dragged so savagely? If at all you had to tell me something, you could have waited till the evening and talked in private. What's the meaning of this shocking behaviour, that too in Shyam's presence? You didn't even realize that your driver was there. How dare you humiliate me in public?'

'As you dare to meet others behind my back.'

'What…? Whom do I meet hiding from you … who with? You know about all my friends. You've met all of them. They all come here and I talk to them in front of you.'

'Did you tell me that you would meet Shyam today … in the park and at this hour?'

'Was it worth telling you about? Do we inform everybody about every trivial matter?'

'I don't come in the category of *everybody*. I am your *husband*.'

'Did you ever tell me before that you didn't like me meeting others?'

'You ought to realize it yourself. If it's necessary to hear from me, then listen. *You will have nothing to do with Anant, Shyam, and Arvind*. You won't meet them anymore.'

'Why?'

'You know very well why. Shyam purchased curtains with ringing bells for his house and got similar ones for you, which you hung in our house. The pen gifted by him … and this watch you always keep hooked on your wrist. No need….'

In a flash, he caught her hand and, regardless of causing any injury or abrasions, he yanked the watch away from her wrist. Suvarna kept shrieking, 'These are my things. Who are you to take them away?'

'If not for you, for the world outside I am your husband. And further … this digital calendar which you keep near your pillow, rather you sleep with, I know Arvind had brought it from abroad.'

'So what…? If they give me presents, I too can reciprocate. When I go abroad, I too will bring something for them. Don't you yourself do all this for your friends?'

'And those sentimental talks. What Anant writes about you. That letter which was there in your office cupboard … what about it?'

'You carried out a search during my absence?'

'I've also heard all that you talk on phone … all that muck that goes on between you people.'

'How could you have stooped so low, Ramesh?'

'*You* should be asking *yourself* this! How could *you* have fallen so low!'

'I've been like this from the very beginning. Have I ever been without friends? And all with your knowledge, all known to you. Earlier, you had never objected to it. All this is the feudal mentality of you men; always on the lookout to humiliate women. You will always see something sinister in a woman's relationships. I've never hidden from you that I give importance to my friends. They contribute so much in my life. I'm proud of them….'

'Now onwards, this is not going to continue. I've been rather too lenient, too liberal.'

'Am I an animal? I'm a human being. I too can have my needs, my desires.'

'Obviously you must be entertaining wicked thoughts, as also your friends, who despite being married, chase women like you.'

'Oh, no! Ramesh, you have such a dirty mind! I never realized it. How filthy is your thinking! A person like you can't even imagine how much they add to my life. I'm not going to abandon the way I have adopted. I'll meet them, meet them a hundred times. Let me see what you can do. You've already done what you wanted to.'

'Shut up!' Ramesh barked and, grinding his teeth, he stepped forward and gave a resounding slap on Suvarna's cheek, which made her recoil.

'Oh, you brute!' she could but shriek. It was the first time in her life that Ramesh, or anybody for that matter, had raised a hand on her, had treated her so savagely.

'This pen and this watch, this calendar and the letter – all these sweet remembrances of yours will remain in my custody. And from now on, you *will not accept* any gift from anyone. I am serious!'

Is this Ramesh … he slapped her?

Suvarna stood still, looking straight at Ramesh. Where has that gentle person gone who was virtually her yes-man, who respected her in every which way? Was that simplicity, that straightforwardness a mere mask? Behind the mask lurked a callous, cunning fellow and she had been living with this monster for years. He's the guy she sleeps with night after night, who she's borne two children! Is he the same person whose parents had come with the proposal of marriage, accepting which she hadn't so much obliged them as she had done a favour to him! That boy in college who dared not raise his eyes to meet her gaze or look at her … now bullying her, beating her! Is he the very person who she thought she loved?

Without saying a word, she came out to the veranda. The structure of the house, in front and on the flanks solid walls of concrete, brick, and stone. The lush green of the creepers covers them here and there but fails to hide their bareness. These hard and solid walls are privy to the goings-on within.

The scorching sun spread out on the lawn, as if brimming full in a bowl whose cool green bottom offered no respite from the heat. All around was the pervading desolation of the afternoon, engulfing the lane outside and the trees in the surroundings.

The plants withering in the heat stood silent, and somewhere in their midst she too kept standing.

No further interaction took place between them. That night, Suvarna slept in a separate room. How can one sleep beside such a person? Now she has to ponder if she can live in the same house as Ramesh. When he would touch her or speak to her, will it be possible to forget the ingrained wickedness of this person?

Next morning, after sending the children to school, she said to Ramesh at breakfast in a cool and balanced voice,

'I'm thinking of leaving the house. I can't live with you. I have a job. I can take care of myself as also the children.'

Ramesh said nothing. He got up and went into his room. It appeared as if, like any other husband, he was taking Suvarna's ultimatum as the usual empty threat given by sulking wives to go to their mothers' houses.

Soon he returned and said, 'Do you see this....' He had a revolver in hand. 'If you think that, leaving me, you will get hooked up with one of those three scoundrels, think again! Don't take this as an empty threat of a mulish fellow. I am warning you, I'll blow your brains out. Those fellows too, I can end a life like this....' he snapped his fingers.

Where life itself is of no worth, there's no question of any value or civility. How suddenly Ramesh has flung his disguise aside and shown his real face ... of a ruthless, heartless cop. This was a typical modus operandi of the police: carry out the raid when it's least expected and surround from all sides. So he got her phone tapped, in her absence took her key and carried out a stealthy search in her office, in his capacity as her husband took possession of her things and attempted to corner her with Shyam, all this in such a manner as though you are carrying out an official investigation, regardless that this concerns human beings dear to you, more so your wife. And now this revolver.

'This is blackmail,' Suvarna said.

'You may think whatever you want ... but take it for sure that you have to *live with me, on my terms*.'

She got up knowing it was futile to continue to talk with such a person.

ꟹ

The day Suvarna reached her office after completing the training, an apparently ruffled Shyam Mohan also arrived there. He had been counting the days – this would have delighted Suvarna, but today she could not extend even a bland welcome to Shyam. With utmost difficulty, she dragged out a 'hello', which was so faint that it might not have reached Shyam at all.

Shyam sat down before her, both looking at each other with a hollow expression. Like two scarecrows facing each other in a field. Suvarna is trying to find her old friend in Shyam. What has that incident – where Shyam was not to blame at all – done that suddenly he has become a stranger?

'Was there a fight that day in your house?'

'No,' she lied in the blinking of an eye.

'Good. All's well that ends well. I was under the impression then that Ramesh has come to wish me, he will sit down, have some sweets, and return. Had I been in his place, I would have done that. If at all he wanted to take you along, he should have made some excuse and then discuss at home whatever he wanted to. He behaved so boorishly outside, and at home, nothing, no reaction. Well, never mind, it happens sometimes. We lose control.'

Suvarna was silent.

'I'm sorry that all this happened because of me. Had I not been so keen to meet you that day, neither would I have gone there nor would Ramesh have got an excuse to treat you like this.'

Suvarna continued to keep quiet.

'Ramesh Bhai must have been furious!'

'He doesn't want me to meet you, Anant, or Arvind.'

'Ramesh should understand that we are educated people. All this passes in our society. People even dance with one another's wives. Husband and wife can't be together at every place.'

'Ramesh's complaint is that he can't move around with Mrs Shyam Mohan as you can with me.'

'If they were to move together, I would have no objection. If my wife is not the outgoing type, what can I do? Let Ramesh come and strike up a friendship with her; like between you and me.'

Suvarna said nothing. She felt as though she'd been speaking for quite some time and was now tired of it. What mudslinging they were indulging in, like children playing a game of throwing muck at each other. Shyam came back to that very matter that she was trying to distance herself from. This subject alone might remain a talking point between them for a number of days. She is developing a kind of dislike for Shyam. Is it only because she was with Shyam when that incident happened, or is it because she has been hearing from Ramesh unflattering comments about Shyam for some days? Whichever of the two, it is wrong. But something has definitely changed. She doesn't want to be with Shyam, though he is not to blame.

'If you agree, I can go and talk to Ramesh to clear up any misunderstanding.'

'No need. You can't knock sense into somebody. It should come from within.'

'I feel Ramesh must have realized his mistake. He'll understand. Don't get upset. No need to take Ramesh's behaviour seriously. Such things happen, buddy. Now be cheerful … come on!'

Shyam's gravity vanished soon, as if a cluster of light clouds just passed over a habitation. His old familiar face had reappeared in no time – laughing every moment, treating everything as a joke. How easy … Suvarna kept watching him in surprise! Could she, in this light-hearted manner, wish away whatever Ramesh had done? Had something like this happened to Shyam, would he have laughed it off? Even if it can be laughed away, is it right to do so? Even if something horrendous happens, just dust it away. Can it be done? Should it be done? How abjectly demeaning and compromising this culture is!

'If, however, you want to act according to Ramesh's wishes, I won't stop you. Why should anyone come between husband and wife?' Getting up from his seat, Shyam said, 'But can you change yourself now at Ramesh's bidding after having spent half your life?'

'No harm trying. But I'm not going to do anything of that sort. Don't know what I am going to do. Just leave me be.'

'You mean you'll be *out of circulation*?'

It was a cliché that Suvarna herself employed quite often. Whenever she had to be away for a few days, or for some reason she wasn't in a position to meet her friends, she would inform everyone beforehand that she would be out of circulation till a certain date … but today the expression pinched her. How demeaning, as if she turned herself into a coin or an object. It was crystal clear that it couldn't describe Suvarna today. She longs to be all by herself, like the sudden desire to be in a sequestered place after passing the day in the hurly-burly of an overcrowded city.

Suvarna just responded with a slight movement of her head and gave a faint smile. What does it matter how Shyam interprets it!

Suvarna used to think that life is for mirth and merriment. Soak inwardly the beauty of the world and cheerfully share it with others. Everyone has something to give and, by the same token, wants to get something in return too. Give-and-take is the very essence of life. No big deal if in order to achieve this, a little bit of sensuality creeps in … after all, they are simply taboos. Take from everyone and enlarge the realm of your experiences. How very small happens to be a person's private world … what's the fun in living like a frog, hopping within the narrow confines of a well? So Suvarna would instantly detect some good in a person and let herself be drawn towards him. So long as there is give-and-take of the good, the relationship has significance. The moment negativity creeps in, it is time to separate.

Suvarna continued to float undeterred, and all along simultaneously took care of Ramesh and his needs. But it all came a cropper like a house of cards felled by a puff of breath. Now, no more will he be the earlier Ramesh, nor will she be able to float free like before.

How fast she was walking and where has she landed! Now what ... who are with her? She could talk to Ramesh about anyone, but who to talk to about Ramesh? Even if she takes somebody into confidence, won't it be humiliating? There was a time when she felt she was surrounded by friends. How brimful was her world! But a solo incident shattered everything. Comprised of these very people, this constellation has come down with a loud thud, as if the canopy stretched above turned out to be mere mist; it vanished in the heat of a sunbeam. Who can she look up to? A scene looms in front ...

Suvarna is running inside a circular area in which people are standing scattered – Arvind, Shyam, Anant, Ramesh, and some others. While running around in circles, she tripped and fell down. She is looking up to see who will come forward to help. No one moves ... the moment she fell, they turned into statues. They will come to life when she gets up on her own and resumes running. But how to get up? Who will lend her support? What else has she done but run? Has the running given her anything that could help her now? Neither has she cared to grow within something that would prop her up.

Emptiness … where once it used to be full to the brim … now such vacuum that even air doesn't stay there. Suvarna is rolling down and down … within herself, in sheer darkness … like a stone slipping down a steep incline.

While in the veranda, Suvarna saw me coming. She looked at me with a blank expression … like a host sees a person who drops in at an odd hour and whose visit is of little consequence. Glancing just once in my direction, she got busy with her activities. She was talking to her children and their tutor. I was coming to her house after quite some time. All these days I couldn't talk to her on phone either. Phone calls from her had stopped. When I rang her up, she would mumble a few words and, saying she would call later, just hang up. Then there would be no call from her. As before, I took her indifference in its stride, thinking that if she is happy about keeping distance from me, I too should get used to it. But then, amid my small-town mindset, a ray of hope began to flicker – she might be in need of your help!

She went inside even after seeing me. The tutor was leaving, the children had dispersed. When I reached the veranda, there was no one there. I could hear voices coming from inside; she was giving instructions to Ramu. I rang the bell.

She came out after a few minutes. Dressed in a yellow saree-blouse, she looked thinner, face looking a tad weary and withered, as if a veneer of sadness had got stuck there. Seeing me she didn't say anything, just looked on, that too in an indifferent manner. Earlier, the welcome used to be a warm 'hi'.

'Have you been ill?' I asked her.

'Going to the Florists' Festival. Children were insisting. Ramesh is there already.' She had a card in her hand with which she was fanning herself.

'It's okay. I'll leave. Could you give me that magazine?'

'Magazine? Which one?'

'The one you had borrowed for the article titled "Modern and Eternal Values". You'd told me you had read it and I could take the magazine back any time.'

She appeared to be utterly confused. She was trying to remember but of little avail. Or was lost in a larger context.

'Do you want it today, right now?'

'Don't bother. You can look for it later. A friend of mine is here, only for four days. He asked for it, that's why ....'

'I'll search ... have to look for it.'

She looked here and there, fidgety, sort of helpless. What a contrast between her former image – a living picture of panache and confidence – and her present one, a plant standing on a single thin root, shaking ominously in a strong wind and in imminent danger of being uprooted any moment.

Emerging out of the veranda, we stood there for some time facing each other. The same tall figure, fair skinned, beautiful, but a little withered. When she comes out to go to the office after getting ready, how fresh she looks, generating, as it were the ambience of spring. But today, only a small lean *amaltas* plant, almost bereft of life.

'How are you?' Her enquiry sounded so distant and diffident, shorn of any genuine wish to know, that there was no need to respond. Her face, which used to undulate pleasantly with myriad waves of expression, was totally blank today, as if a stony coating was fast approaching from all sides to cover it. The emptiness in her eyes was even more pronounced like that of a long deserted dwelling. She was looking in my direction with unseeing eyes. Maybe she was seeing beyond me or she was seeing nothing at all.

'You don't ring up these days?' I asked.

'No … what?' her fractured response making no sense.

She stepped forward signifying that any exchange of news about each other was of no consequence to her. The angel had flown away and we both – probably me alone – were searching the direction it had gone. Not she, only a shell was moving. She was walking as if in a trance. That stony look on her face presaged some illness. Such a layer is seen creeping on a dying face.

The children had come out. They all proceeded towards the car. First the children sat, followed by her. She continued to look at me with blank eyes. When the car started, she seemed to remember something and made a feeble attempt to wave, but by then the car had surged ahead.

Florists' Festival. Ramesh the chief guest, Suvarna and children given a special welcome. There was a time when being accorded such importance pleased her no end. Now all that is looking hollow. She went wherever the event organizers took her and sat down wherever asked to. On one side Ramesh, on the other children. She in between. Ramesh's face glowing with pride … see … I can give you this – so much respect and honour.

The venue wore a festive look. The ambience embellished and made fragrant with a riot of colours of the flowers on display and their scent.

'Mummy, see those yellow flowers. What's their name?' The younger child wants to know.

'No idea, dear.'

'So beautiful, aren't they?'

'Yes.'

Ramesh gets up and goes over to the children's side, and keeps them engaged in conversation. 'It's a festival of meeting, of friendship ….' he is telling them.

Suvarna doesn't talk, even with the children – Ramesh thinks – sitting here in a sulk, just as she does at home, no regard for his position. Everyone is watching us, at least here she should …

He had given her too much freedom. Suvarna took undue advantage of it. Instead of being grateful, she began to consider Ramesh a moron. She used to order him about as if he were simply a clerk in her office. The more Ramesh acquiesced, the more dictatorial she became. She would not brook any opposition. At last, Ramesh had to become strict. He placed such incriminating proof before Suvarna that all her bravado vanished … now, only Ramesh's writ would run. Ramesh knows Suvarna has had a rude shock. And this is what he wanted. If, all of a sudden, you become strict, there is bound to be shock … like a half-asleep sentry having to suddenly stand up ramrod straight. The plan of enforcing strict discipline rests on the notion that you so dominate a person's mind so that he or she is unable to think at all. Executing such a plan requires full preparation. Strictness is essential; if you aren't strict, you are considered a weakling. Suvarna is educated, has a good income, but it doesn't mean that she can indulge in any activity, even those that make Ramesh bow his head in shame. If she had no education, she wouldn't have gone to office … where's the need? What does Ramesh get out of it? An office job gives an opportunity to a woman to flirt. While the poor hubby sits cuckolded at home and you…! Damn it! A wife isn't meant to be shared.

Suvarna says she is not a property. If, after marriage, the husband alone has a right over her, what else is she but piece of property. Mutual love and caring alone entitle a person to exercise the right … bullshit! They have been living together for so many years. Suvarna never thought all this before. Since Anant – that son of a bitch – became her friend, Suvarna's mind has been bristling with crazy ideas. Mrs Ramesh, you have a home, you have chosen to live in this home; there's your husband and children, look after them, make them happy … this should be the sole aim of your life. What else do you search frantically? Is it an era of Heer-Ranjha or Sohni-Mahiwal? In this age of science, only the sick indulge in such things. Let's live for ourselves alone, better our financial position, and ensure our advancement as well as that of our children. What else is needed? And the lovey-dovey business, in any case, goes on at night between us.

And Urvashi?

It is what gets Ramesh's goat. Suvarna knows only this much that Ramesh and Urvashi are colleagues. Suvarna couldn't even have any suspicion. Ramesh is not given to such obsession that he is with wife and his mind is fantasizing about somebody else. Urvashi, too, has a similar temperament. If both have the mood, time, and opportunity, they would make love and fling it away from their minds soon thereafter. Why should something physical stick to the mind endlessly ... this is modern thinking. Ramesh and Urvashi are friends, so they take care of each other ... in this matter too. Till Urvashi doesn't get married, this will go on. Later, they won't need it, so the matter would rest there. Ramesh knows that Suvarna doesn't have relations of this type with anyone, but they could develop later on. Suvarna lacks the subtlety to get out without any hassle as Ramesh can do. What Suvarna was doing was fraught with danger. It could have triggered a sequence of events leading to a lifelong entanglement. Okay, you may flirt with ten persons with impunity, but all this affair of heart, so sublime looking in reel life, can spell disaster in real life by ending up in lifelong involvement. Ramesh has taken a decision after careful thought that all this nonsense should be put an end to, so that Suvarna returns to the straight path. Those who are exerting a bad influence on her should be got rid of. She may make friends with others, but not with this gang of three. Ramesh is tough – once a decision is taken, it's final. Changing a decision or any indecisiveness hasn't been a part of his training, as an officer of the Indian Police Service.

Suvarna is half asleep. A medley of sights and sounds – colours, flowers, and music – is passing or resonating before her. The sound of music is stretched over her like a sheet. Wrapped in it, Suvarna is sleeping.

Pulling up a chair in the veranda, Suvarna sat down in a corner there, looking into the horizon. These days, this is her daily routine after returning from office. She will occupy a chair in this very corner and continue sitting. Lacklustre eyes watching activities going on in front – swaying trees, rustling of leaves, birds flying about sometimes on sensing some danger and sometimes out of necessity, gradual receding of the sun, bright colours changing into greys and blacks.

Voices emanate from this kaleidoscopic scene and crawl on the infinite emptiness inside and outside Suvarna. For some time, it appears that something is in the offing and taking shape. Suvarna will recognize it at the very first sight. Yes, this is it … here I am! But the very instant Suvarna attempts to grasp it, everything vanishes. The feeble voices are lost in the wilderness within her. Suvarna is left waiting endlessly, watching helplessly.

She is making all efforts to come out. Earlier she had turned into a block of ice – nothing getting inside, no feeling. Then slowly and gradually, outward things began to register. Since she started sleeping in a separate room away from Ramesh, she's noticed that the children have started staring at Mummy-Papa, questions writ large on their faces. Their eyes try to probe; they must have smelt that all is not well, something is wrong. It isn't fair that when her discord is with Ramesh, her children should suffer. Until she reaches some decision, she will have to show that everything is normal, just like before. Though she feels it in her bones that never will it be the same again. Yet, for the time being, she should sleep in the room where she slept earlier. For appearances sake, she'd talk a couple of times to Ramesh in the presence of the children, though the channel of communication between them has broken down completely.

She doesn't want to meet anyone. She goes to the office so that she could remain outside home … also that she might get time to think and come to some decision. She's sent word to all that she won't be able to meet for some days owing to her busy schedule, and nobody should phone her either. Only official phones and official work and discussion over official matters. Straight from office to home, and then getting busy with household chores. She doesn't even feel like talking to the children.

She has to take pills to steady her nerves … hasn't as yet come out of the trauma. The only thing that has come about is that the incident that earlier appeared to have happened only in dream can now be seen as having happened in reality. For the first time in her life, terrible frustration has overtaken her; doesn't leave her for even an instant. Suvarna knows very well that she alone has to seek her deliverance, ponder over her situation, and reach some conclusion.

Ramesh has intelligence but not the capacity to think. Suvarna is not just a housewife but a working woman. Even if Ramesh is aware of this, he lacks the sensitivity to understand what all it implies. Suvarna is bound to have a separate life. There would be some officers who she has to give special regard.…She is most likely to have a different set of friends. And as for the basic fact that she is a different person, has her own personality – Ramesh will, in all probability, rubbish it all as hogwash. In his assessment, it suffices that she is someone's wife, her husband is a high-ranking official, she has a decent house, and they enjoy a good reputation in society. Ramesh can never understand that a person may have needs beyond these goodies. Human body itself can have so many dimensions … Ramesh mustn't be knowing where and at what points Suvarna was left thirsty. From Suvarna's beauty flows poetic outpourings, but as far as Ramesh is concerned, she is simply a machine to be run or switched off at will.

What does Suvarna want from life?

Maybe her basic urge is to live an unfettered life, though she has no inkling as to what that sort of living is all about. She thinks she'll find out in course of time. If she remains confined within the four walls, she'll never be able to discover it. Which is why she has relationships of varied sorts with different persons. Anant says the most precious thing in life is love. But isn't love there just to open a new window, to add something further to life? The real thing is to live life – all roads lead to it.

Suvarna wants to live on her terms, a full rich life. These relationships of hers are necessary, because they make her feel, make her breathe life. She's able to get along with different persons in different modes. Suvarna wants people to regard her as an above-average intelligent woman and as an individual who is free in all respects and is self-dependent. It is immaterial that she is female and the one opposite her is a male. If a little bit of that does come in, it is of no consequence. All her relationships began with mutual respect and admiration for qualities in each other, but God knows why, after traversing some distance in a relationship, somehow this male–female angle creeps in. The man before her starts admiring her beauty and she relishing it. With some, she does go a step or two further. Then Suvarna has to exert to protect herself even while keeping the company of that person. With Ramesh also, it is the same; here she has to guard her individuality too.

Ramesh's discomfiture is that even after having her as his wife, he hasn't succeeded in possessing her completely. But can anyone ever possess another person in this manner, and if it all he succeeds, isn't it any less than homicide? Then why this lust for possession?

Sometimes she curses herself that if this was going to be her thinking, why did she let herself be tied in wedlock? But at the age of twenty, twenty-one, one hardly knows the consequences of lifelong bonding. Now, at this stage, however much she may rubbish these ties, they will remain transfixed and continue to prod her. In fact, the way she wants to come upfront and belie them is something that will never be allowed. In a society, where people start chasing a girl on seeing her alone, she can negate these ties only in a hush-hush manner. Many a time, she has longed to wander alone on streets in the night's darkness, run on the grass while drenched in rain, venture out alone on long journeys, stroll on deserted paths for hours together, or jump into a river and swim and float at will. But could she fulfil even one of these wishes? Why is it so that even for communion with nature, a woman needs the company of a man … if Ramesh has neither any interest nor leisure, then somebody else's company. Often this has happened that while strolling in a grove of trees with someone, she has wished that her companion keep mum and let her directly commune with the trees.

Ramesh doesn't like her relationships. She mustn't mix with certain persons … why? This will make him happy … means she isn't even his wife but a bonded maid. Ramesh's contention would be that he has no relations with any woman except his wife … so. Unquestioned fidelity!

But what sort of fidelity is it which leaves no scope to an individual to be faithful to one's own self? Why do we want in return the same that we give? If she were to observe unflinching fidelity to Ramesh, she would be finished! Ramesh has been loyal to her; she too has responded with her love – better than his, though he doesn't deserve it. And what has Suvarna got in the bargain? Security, the status of a high-ranking man's wife, prestige in society! What sort of society? That arid society where you are under compulsion to always look complacent and happy, to needlessly converse on mundane topics … where there are only acquaintances, no friends, where, on the face of it, there's a flowing stream of happiness but no feel for real bliss. Stark wilderness of a desert, but people in colourful balloons! …. There must have been some cogent reason that, fed up with her boring life, Suvarna kept getting into those relationships that are today Ramesh's eyesore and totally unacceptable to him. Wasn't it owing to these relationships that she could till now bear her boredom and love Ramesh as well…?

Now, reaching this point, where there are neither those relationships nor any love for Ramesh, she feels totally devastated. Did her identity rest on these attachments only … without them, was she a nobody, sapped of will to reassert her individuality? How fragile and feeble is the cobweb of delusions that we wrap ourselves with!

Suvarna didn't realize that the sun had receded long back, darkness looming over her, yet she kept sitting. Should she get up … what would she do after …

Invoking Strength

Seeing me suddenly in her room, she got rattled. She got up instantly and, going to the window, peered outside. Some unknown fear had dimmed the glow on her face.

The winter wasn't over as yet, but in the warmth of the sprawling sun, there was a hint of the impending summer. The pond across the outer wall of the office was dry. The dirty moss on the hard bottom was scattered about like greenish mud, somewhere thickly spread, somewhere sparser, wet and sticky.

'Did you see Ramesh's car outside?' she asked, while still standing at the window.

'I didn't pay attention. Even otherwise, I can't recognize correctly, nor do I remember the registration number. But why…?'

After giving a once-over to the number of cars parked across the wall, she returned and sat down on her chair.

'Why have you come? Hadn't I told you that I wouldn't be able to meet you for some days?'

'Okay, I'll go. I came because I couldn't help it. Three or four months have passed, but no news about you. I had an uncanny feeling. The unusual urgency on your part to disconnect phone calls, that day your behaviour in your house! Felt something was amiss. I know my limits. Neither am I going to interfere needlessly, nor will I want to know what you are reluctant to reveal.'

'Why do you care so much for me?'

Her voice didn't sound emotional at all. On the contrary, it appeared to be in a complaining mode that so much concern was a burden.

'These days Ramesh keeps hovering about in the vicinity, keeping a vigil as to who visits me. He stole my keys and searched my almirahs. He gets my phone calls tapped. Anant, I'd never imagined that Ramesh could stoop so low. Even now, sometimes it looks like a dream and not reality. He knew right from the beginning about my socializing. He knows about each and every relationship of mine … now he prohibits me from meeting you, Arvind, and Shyam….'

The dam had burst. It surprised me not one whit. This was a crisis waiting to happen. It was merely a question of 'when'.

Long repressed feelings of Ramesh at last came to a boil and spewed out with the same force as had kept them suppressed all this while.

'Anant, you should leave … he can drop in anytime. Nowadays, he makes a sudden surprise appearance. He says if no one is prohibited from coming here, then why should he be. He will come here and sit down as if he were on a police beat.'

'Did you tell Shyam and Arvind?' I asked.

'They already know. On his birthday, Shyam came to my training institute. Now, was it worth making an issue of? Ramesh reached there and created a scene. Dragged me from there, forced me to get into his car, and brought me home … as if I had no dignity.'

'You should have explained to him.'

'Explained? He resorts to violence. Twice he has slapped me. Anant, all these years I'd been living with a beast.'

She broke down. The precious possession that she had preserved close to her heart turned out to be a balloon. It just popped at a mere touch. She had been severely traumatized, lost her bearings, and was now picking up the pieces.

'Look here, as regards Ramesh's feelings, one can divine the cause.'

'But what was so new? What had happened that made him act in such a brutish manner? I've had friends right from the very beginning. When I made my first friend, Ramesh should have stopped me then. What am I to do now, Anant…?'

'What do Arvind and Shyam say?'

'They also felt very bad at Ramesh's behaviour. Both were ready to talk to Ramesh individually. I'm proud of my friends in this respect. I asked them myself not to, prohibited them from coming here or ringing up. I don't want any untoward incident to happen. You very well know I'd never before experienced such boorishness in my life.

His violent behaviour is unbearable. Ramesh has become so unpredictable. I don't trust him at all. That day, he dragged me in the presence of a driver. What unflattering ideas must have crossed the driver's mind that such unseemly activities take place among the so-called elite. I didn't have the faintest idea that Ramesh was so stupid. By humiliating his wife publicly, he was only degrading himself … and this happens to be the man who I've loved all these years.'

She was boiling with rage, as she hadn't till now had anyone to confide her terrible experience in. Even normally, she would remain stuck up with the immediate present, be it some office matter or some niggling problem of health; while the recent incident was no small matter, especially for a person like her whose life had flowed on merrily without let or hindrance. Maybe, barring films, she had never before seen such domestic rift and ruckus.

'Anant, you better go now….'

What a contrast! Suvarna of my early days with her – picture of supreme confidence that she didn't do anything hidden from Ramesh and could even tell him that she liked me – and the present Suvarna, so diffident, cowering, and quailing. Was her earlier courage just a sham?

I didn't heed to her advice to go away. All that she accepted as gospel truth and was also visible as such in her living had come down crashing. I wasn't in any position to help her, but at least could be by her side for some time.

'I think this is the time when you should look for courage within instead of giving into edginess, hasty and thoughtless reaction, or inferiority complex. Perhaps, your closest relationship is with me. And, as for me, this is so sacred that I'll have no hesitation in admitting it to Ramesh or anybody else. If I worship somebody in my heart, how can it be termed as shameful? And when love gets elevated to the level of worship, how blissful life becomes! Just give it a thought. Can there be anything disgraceful about it? To me, this is the very acme of life which I have not achieved yet, but I do manage to touch sometimes....'

Deeply moved ... she was in a state of near-trance, as if she had traversed quite a distance even away from herself. The scratches of humiliation, tension, and helplessness that had been overlaying her face minutes before seemed to be on the wane, and now it looked washed clean ... melting in an unknown sweetness ... her eyes suffused with myriad hues of dreams unseen. How could such an individual be treated the way she had been by Ramesh?

The glow of inner beauty couldn't stay long on her face. The web of her perplexities resurfaced there, as was evident from the crisscrossing taut veins. Then I realized how severely her recent ordeal had devastated her from within.

'If your relations with Ramesh weren't of that sort before marriage, they could have evolved post marriage ... such as would have sunk into each other's soul. Since this didn't happen, your marriage remained simply a cover. Conventional wisdom led you to believe that you two are husband and wife. The birth of children further strengthened this perception not only in the immediate family but also socially. That said, what was most essential in such a relationship – the emotional, the bonding of souls – was conspicuous by its absence....

Sometimes I feel all your relationships are deficient ... they exist only piecemeal; they do not fill you completely.'

She began to look beyond me. She did so only when she was listening very carefully, but if you looked at her, you would form a contrary impression.

Neither of us uttered a single word for the next few moments. I was waiting for her response and she continued struggling inside.

'May I talk it out with Ramesh?' I broke the stifling silence.

'Oh!' she seemed to wake up. 'What did you say?'

'Will my talking have any effect?'

'With whom ... with Ramesh? No, no. Just futile! He threatens me with his revolver. Sometimes, I think from where a man gets the right to treat his wife so savagely, maybe a goner like me. Or any type, for that matter. Now the question is: how can I live with this sort of man?'

'Such steps can't be taken without courage. For this to happen, you will have to strengthen your moral fibre. Where there is belief, it is easy. Else, you have to search those beliefs for which you are prepared to do or die.'

'Which such beliefs are mine, Anant?' she asked.

This was the height of helplessness that all of a sudden surfaced over her sagging morale. Defeatist attitude and stark frustration were already there in her speech; it was an inner cry which came out now. Suvarna was looking at me … forlorn, helpless, vulnerable, as though nothing lay before her but a vast stretch of barrenness, not even a stump to get a leg-up. Those eyes which seldom shed tears, never before others, were getting misty. Again and again she would be on the verge of crying, but somehow managed to collect herself. Had she been alone, she would have cried hoarse, wept her heart out, as she had never done in her life.

I was filled with remorse. This wasn't the time to weigh her down with high-sounding sermonizing. I ought to have just shared her pain and anguish. That said, this was the time for her to ponder over and just when such thoughts could be of some help.

'He says if I go away leaving him, he will kill me. No way will he let me leave him.'

'And you got scared. It's here we know what our culture, our upbringing has made of us. We feel scared only when we let our beliefs go for a toss, which saps our confidence and mental strength. I fully don't know what your values and beliefs are. You have to look for them within yourself … and you will surely find them. Everyone has them; what is needed is to find them, identify them, and have faith in them. And this happens only in moments of upheaval and crisis. We shouldn't take any decision under duress, but only in the light of our beliefs.'

I wasn't inciting her, my ire was against that lame duck of a person moulded by our city culture; he shows that he is capable of grappling with high-octane issues, but when confronted with testing times, is ready to make compromises using some grand reason for this abject surrender. I knew she wouldn't do anything. For a few days, she would grumble and remain churlish and, eventually, return to square one where she is not to defy but to act and comply with Ramesh's diktats. For outsiders and for herself too, her stock reasoning would be that after all, children's interests couldn't be overlooked.

'When my mother learns of it, she won't be able to tolerate it. She is so cultured. This is the hitch in such matters. If you show defiance, you're courting more disrepute for yourself. Everyone can't be shameless like Ramesh.'

'If it's hollow inside, what's the use of window dressing outside? What's come over us that ignoring the essential, we take pains to keep up appearances?'

'Now you should go.'

'Why, are you so scared?'

'No, there's something like civility. I don't want any scene here in the office. I have the least trust in Ramesh now. No knowing what he might do and when.'

'All right. If possible, try to remember that you aren't alone. All those who are going through such distress, they are all with us at this moment, no matter if we are unacquainted with them. Both of us have our crosses to bear, you … and … I. If you so desire….'

'I understand….' she said, while placing her palm in my hands. 'I get strength from you. It often appears you're articulating my feelings.'

While leaving, I placed my hand on her head … invoking divine help for her. The sort of person she was, it was most unlikely that she would ever take anybody's help; she would go on suffering extreme torment within till she herself came to a decision. But has she the necessary strength to take a final call? Ramesh's action was atrocious. Do we treat somebody we love so wickedly? Where is love there? At stake, there is only one thing, namely the prestige of being a beautiful woman's husband. It has to be saved, as if it was some throne!

12 February 1980

We are getting more and more hollow, as we want to skip suffering because of our insatiable lust for pleasure … and to justify our hedonistic craving, we put forth myriad strands of logic. Our upper class and the upper-middle class imitating it are losing the capacity to feel love. Don't fall in love because there is suffering in it … so don't do anything at all for anybody because there is a spot of unnecessary bother in it. At the end of the day, a person nursing such an attitude is left holding a lemon, because his sole passion is in acquiring … success ever and everywhere. Every moment in a tearing hurry to grab something. Civilization developed with man's desire to do something for the other. If, however, the present covet-and-snatch syndrome goes on unabated, humanity will soon descend to that level when every self-seeker engaged in the rat race will eye every other person with suspicion and scars; their insecurity will compel them to cocoon themselves in a protective shell. What a contrast between the sacrificing attitude of love and this demeaning cut-throat rivalry. Yet, knowingly, man is treading on a devious path.

The transience of things in the flux of time is in itself a great suffering, and since life in totality is transient, the core of it is only suffering. Suvarna is tasting her share of suffering now … she is sure to emerge cleansed from this crucible.

Is cold detachment getting the better of me? Detachment for everything … even for Suvarna? It isn't so … except that I have come to believe that life can't be taken in halves; it has to be taken in its entirety; so good or bad, pleasure or pain – all should be equally acceptable.

So much has gone over us; some over us together, some separately. But if she is beside me, I'll experience the fullness of life as before … how her nearness expands me individually.

Similar probing eyes, same type of fascinated look …

Suvarna is beautiful … she tries to remember, as if some distant bells ring, and it is some long past event … yes, people look at her this way for this very reason.

He has come along with Suvarna's colleague Janaki. Right now, Janaki is important. After Janaki introduces him to Suvarna, she will be cast aside like an unwanted prop or ladder. Isn't it so, Mr…?

Round figure, a little below average height, and an expanding waistline, as if reaching a point, the body simply refused moving upwards; its growth then developed into thick muscles sideways. He, however, keeps them tight to look smart. An articulate talker. His lack of good looks more than compensated by his overall intelligence and smartness.

'If we think that nothing can be done, if the intellectuals also get afflicted with this defeatist outlook, there is no hope left for the country. But let's ponder why it is so. The same persons do wonders on going abroad, while they were good-for-nothing fellows here. It means our people aren't inferior in any way. The fault lies in the system. We have to visit institutions and help them in bringing about the desired change in the system. After all, it is they who have to do this, but we will guide them as experts....'

Bubbling over with enthusiasm, he also knows how to establish a new institution. With details, he underlines that the proposed research organization will have people of high calibre and it will approach big industrial houses and offer its services to them. Problems will be studied in a scientific manner and, likewise, credible solutions suggested. Funds will come from this source and that, persons manning the institution will have such and such qualifications, and in the beginning there will be a blitzkrieg of publicity to give us a resounding start. We will acquire land in this manner, and such will be the building. We will have to keep visiting abroad to update our know-how....

The scheme is attractive. He wants Suvarna's name in the Board of Directors along with some big persons … why? Any special qualification Suvarna possesses? Replies: some enterprising and active workers are needed and she fits the role! Suvarna finds the proposal interesting, starts liking the person after hearing him. Enterprising, emerging from his small narrow world, concerned for the whole country and endeavouring to do something at that level … and this smile, such an integrating smile, slight and delicate … hardly ever seen such a smile that will dissipate his beholders' sourness and overwhelm them with his sweetness. Armed with such a captivating smile, this man can sell anything, be it an idea, a proposal, a product … anything.

Suvarna is getting attracted. Today's pleasant talk does lift her from the doom and gloom of the past few days. There is nothing suspicious about this person; undeterred, she could go a distance with him … she finds herself in a feel-good mode. Even Ramesh won't have any objection about him. Suvarna knows that if she were to loosen up just slightly, the very next day they would become close friends. How very soon life is ready to rise all over again and start racing … it is short, that's why…!

No, no … presently there is country, institution, research, project … a grand plan in the offing. Very soon, all this will be over … what would remain then will be him and me, man and woman. Like drawing the air in, he will start sucking Suvarna into his friendship. How will it be different from what has been happening with her so far? Suvarna will again be seen running about. All these attachments, apparently different from one another on the surface, are terribly one and the same just one layer underneath … they take us far away from ourselves. For the past few days, Suvarna has kept herself away from others so that she could remain with herself.

'I know one music institute. It also started with similar lofty ideals … to awaken the traditions of Indian music among children, and so on so forth. Singers from Bombay were brought for concerts to collect funds. A large plot of land was managed for a music college. In his capacity as principal, a gentleman grabbed a bungalow. You will be surprised to know that all who were associated with the project, including the principal, knew only a smattering of music. At least, some professional musicians could have been inducted into the institute … instead, they unabashedly went on employing relatives.'

Suvarna had flared up abruptly. Even otherwise, these days she cannot talk in a composed way.

'But you will be there in the institution. It'll be in your hands not to allow such malpractices.'

Any other person would have got not only dismayed but also offended to see his proposal being treated in such an offhand manner. The new kid on the block made of sterner stuff isn't ready to give up. Unleashing his bewitching smile and persuasive style, he counters Suvarna's outright rejection and again makes great play of his plan.

'It will depend on us that we take up this as an important project, give it our undivided attention, and not let ourselves be distracted by trivial things. People normally live for themselves only, but we should also contribute to the common good, towards welfare of the public and the country.'

'The trouble is that vested interest always gets into welfare work intended for the public or the country. Governors' wives take up some social service work, for example, helping the disabled persons or other such humanitarian activities, but it doesn't mean that they are really inspired. Rather, they feel happy about showing off their philanthropy. Who does this kind of work for its sake? Those who do, they don't advertise.'

Suvarna is fighting, against herself. She knows she has a weakness for getting involved in some such work. But she also knows that the matter will not rest there; she will be in the company of this man. No one will offer such work to Suvarna for work's sake; she herself has to look for it quietly. Had it been some other time, she would have got involved in this man's proposal, thinking perhaps this is what she's been looking for. But these days, a resolve to change her lifestyle is doggedly taking shape – she will now remain away from others as much as she has remained with them so far – now her sole companion will be herself, just herself. Suvarna should experience this too. Has this change come about owing to Ramesh's shouting and raving? Even if it has, so what; there's always some pretext or reason for any change to come. But the moment she thinks of living away from others, the first in the list of such persons happens to be Ramesh.

The man sitting across hasn't yet accepted defeat. His smile is intact, as wide as before. This man is bound to be successful in life; he possesses an important quality of our times … to keep smiling, come rain, come storm! Even then, Suvarna is firm in her 'no'. Now she should start attempting not to succumb to other's persuasions but to remain steadfast in her resolve. Her drifting hither and yon has taken a heavy toll of her strength, which could not be concentrated at a single point but got dissipated in various directions and hence couldn't be felt even by her. Having squandered her strength in unrewarding distractions, she is feeling completely crushed. Suvarna will have to recoup every ounce of her strength, which only then can prop her up….

Go … friend … go … if we really need each other, we will somehow discover the other. Else, building relationships, like picking differently shaped, coloured stones and pebbles strewn on the path will have nothing but decorative value. Suvarna doesn't need decoration now; she needs strength.

Name which was Lost

Gentle knock on the door.

'Come in' – the very same words that are current and commonplace in an office. After uttering them, Suvarna continued the discussion with her assistant about the file before her.

The door opened with a slight touch. A lady came up to the table quietly and sat down on a vacant chair. The moment Suvarna noticed her, a weird silence seemed to permeate the room. Suvarna kept gazing at the woman, wanting to say something, but couldn't; she remained tongue-tied. At length, she braced herself and told her assistant to come later.

'Please … you may finish,' the lady suggested.

'It's alright. It can wait.'

The assistant got up with a surprised look at the lady. The normal formal atmosphere of the office had suddenly changed. Trying to unravel the 'what' and 'why' of the occurrence, he slowly walked out of the room.

After the assistant's exit, deafening silence hung in the room for sometime; though every object in the room did seem to be saying something – papers lying in front, paperweight, telephone, table lamp ... all of them, especially the whirr of the fan running on slow speed sounding like a groan.

'How are you? What will you have – tea or coffee?'

And without waiting for a reply from the visitor, Suvarna rang the bell for the peon and asked him to get two cups of tea.

The lady, Mrs Shyam Mohan, isn't a stranger to Suvarna. She has met her before two or three times, but her coming like this to the office? During these tumultuous times she is passing through, Suvarna is engulfed with a sense of premonition that something imminent, something untoward is going to happen. Two days ago, Arvind had called her up and told her that Ramesh had met him and warned him not to meet Suvarna, otherwise Ramesh would ensure that his house would also be gripped with the same disharmony that has overtaken Ramesh's house. Arvind, as is his wont, took Ramesh's threat calmly. After Ramesh had left, he rang up Suvarna and asked, 'What do you say?'

'Nothing ... except that right now I can't meet you.' She could tell him this much.

'What should I do?'

'Whatever you think fit.' And she hung up. These days she doesn't feel like talking to anyone, particularly on this subject.

Mrs Shyam Mohan seemed to be slightly subdued. She was not at all what she was when Ramesh and Suvarna had gone to their place, or when she and Shyam had come on a return visit. Neither was Suvarna the same – upbeat as she was on those occasions. That cheerfulness in the ambience … was it owing to those two men?

'How are you?' Suvarna tried to pick up the threads of the conversation.

'Good.'

'We are meeting after a long time.'

'Yes.'

'How is Shyam?'

'You don't know?'

'I haven't met him for quite some time.'

'Why…?'

Suvarna was stumped for a reply. Meanwhile, the bearer brought the tea. Mrs Shyam's question remained hanging in the air, unanswered. Suvarna pulled the tray towards herself, while Mrs Shyam was rotating the ring around her finger.

'Sugar?'

'No please.'

'Absolutely no?'

'Sugar does not agree with me these days. You are yet to reach my age.'

Suvarna shrugged off the remark laughingly, but the embedded barb was a wake-up call. 'Be on your guard.'

'No escape for me either. Sooner or later, have to reach there,' Suvarna said, while pouring tea.

'Not necessarily so, it can be postponed. Why should you age prematurely, like me?'

It appeared futile to further continue with this topic. Whatever is destined is in the hands of nature. No sense in crowing or carping about it.

After pushing the cup towards Mrs Shyam, Suvarna silently began to stir sugar in her cup. The rotating spoon in the cup was generating gentle music to Suvarna's liking. Sometimes, such sounds made by inanimate objects are much sweeter than human voices.

'Mr Ramesh had come to give these.'

Mrs Shyam Mohan took out a watch and a pen from her purse and placed them on the table. A glance and Suvarna turned into a shell … all air seemed suddenly sucked out, she felt faint, weightless for a few seconds. When she got a grip on herself and regained her composure, she glanced at those objects again. How dull they looked, like pieces of junk! That day when Ramesh was flashing them before her with a demonic flourish, they looked menacing. In contrast, when Shyam had first given them to her, they seemed endowed with life and cheer! And today, mere pieces of junk. As though, they had lost their sheen in the intervening period. A sort of staleness emanating from them was spreading across Suvarna's face.

Suvarna felt that she had been driven against a wall. Now all were bent upon mudslinging and throwing muck at her. She collected herself … shook herself hard and told herself, beware, these people will make mincemeat of you.

'So what am I supposed to do?' her voice had a stern note to it.

'These are your things, they were given to you.'

'But Ramesh has returned them … given them back to you.'

'What will I do with them?'

'Hand them over to Shyam.'

'Couldn't you return them to him?'

Suvarna couldn't say anything … how could she say that here lies the rub – Ramesh didn't give her an opportunity. How ironic that the Indian woman has to be a partner in each demeaning act of her husband!

'Actually these things are neither mine nor Ramesh's. Neither did they belong to Shyam after he had given them to you. If you so desire, you can keep them with you.'

Mrs Shyam Mohan's tone was very gentle. Suvarna knew that the family was highly cultured.

'Ramesh also told me to stop Shyam socializing with you. This is causing dissension in your family.'

'Then stop him.'

'I did advise him and he's agreed. He said that he didn't know that Ramesh takes it amiss.'

Suvarna's jaws stiffened … so Shyam's conduct would also be decided by Ramesh. Ramesh's suffering was important, not hers who had relations with Shyam … just because she was a woman!

'You stop Shyam and Ramesh wants to stop me … as if we are mad people … plunderers, out to devastate a whole habitation,' Suvarna exploded suddenly. 'Pray, what have we done to deserve this mudslinging from you people? Are we such irredeemable sinners that reforming us has become an unenviable task for you people? Couldn't you take Ramesh to task and send him packing? He's maligning himself along with his wife and Shyam. Even you're being humiliated.'

Mrs Shyam Mohan got scared. She'd not expected such an outburst. Suvarna's pent-up emotions, kept in check all these days, could not be contained any longer and spewed out with full force.

'How weak-willed women like you are! One man – your husband – explains to you that his relations with me are all right and you accept it. Another man – my husband – gives you some dubious information and, on his say-so, you get busy reforming Shyam as well as me. Is it that you too were harbouring the same dirty thoughts as Ramesh and now you've got a chance to express them…?'

'Had it been so, would I have come to return these things?'

'I don't want these things. Take them away … nor do I see the need to meet Shyam and complete the formality of returning them. It's all so disgusting … these things … Shyam … Ramesh … myself … everything, everyone!'

Mrs Shyam Mohan put back the watch and the pen inside her purse. She wiped the sweat off her face and went out of the room.

The one left behind was Suvarna … enraged, emotionally drained. Her being lay shattered to smithereens and she was at a loss to extricate herself from this intractable mess. An individual – possessed of such a personality as would outshine anyone anywhere – has to stand in the dock before people, as if she were a person of blackened reputation, a thief, a whore. After all, what crime had she committed to earn this ignominy?

All this due to Ramesh … can she still continue to live with such a person?

He's certain to meet Arvind's wife who, too, will come someday to humiliate her. If she were to talk in these people's language, she could ask these wives why they are so weak that they couldn't safekeep their husbands. If she were to descend to Ramesh's level, she could ask him what is it that he couldn't give to his wife – which led her to others.

One question confronts her again and again – how long will it continue like this … how can she live with a man like Ramesh?

She didn't talk to Ramesh after returning home just as she had done that day when she had learnt that Ramesh had been to Arvind, not knowing what he had spoken to him. Ramesh's going to Arvind is to some extent understandable – a jealous husband straight away confronting the man against whom he has a grudge. But going to the wives and through them have Suvarna humiliated, it's surely hitting below the belt! Before resorting to such crudeness, he ought to have spared a thought for Shyam's and Arvind's families. Very nice people they are, and here he's going to their houses and indulging in this mudslinging. Day by day, Ramesh is sinking lower and yet lower. How low will she have to descend with Ramesh, to what extent will she continue to be humiliated by all and sundry? The overriding question is – after all this, can she still love Ramesh … wouldn't her continuing to live with him be a mockery akin to what every second Indian woman takes recourse to? Is Suvarna under any compulsion to do so? Some ways she is certainly different, as she herself has all along believed. What ways …

Sleeping pill, yet no sleep.

How irritated Anant gets, says today's educated city dwellers do their work with doses of Calmpose and go to bed after taking a sleeping pill. They take drugs to enhance their tolerance power, but addiction only makes them weaker and weaker.

Is Suvarna getting weaker, or with the help of these pills somehow managing to keep herself afloat? She does have a purpose – the news of her breakdown should not reach outside, but is it being achieved? She's certainly managed to save herself … but why … for whom … for Ramesh?

By her side, her 'master' is snoring in his sleep!

It has been more than four months, their communication is limited to bare minimum. Ramesh hasn't had the courage to touch her. Means she does have some power … what sort … can't this power be further enhanced? Anant had said that whenever we look for power within, we get it. What's actually needed is to nurture it and be conscious about it.

The dial of the clock on the dressing table is shining … a circle of faint green light, it is past 2 am. Not a wink of sleep as yet, no chance either. She gets up from the bed. The bedroom door remains ajar these days, the children's room opposite it. When she began to sleep here again, Ramesh had tried to close the door like before. Suvarna had put her foot down and shrieked, her voice reaching the children's room – 'The door will remain open … the children should be able to see me.' The children, terribly frightened, were looking at her. Ramesh couldn't close the door even on the following days.

The children are sleeping, blissfully ignorant. But they are aware that what's happening around them is not normal. Nothing is visible to them openly, nor have they any idea that this storm will engulf them too. Carefree they are sleeping – Mummy is nearby, just in front across the open door. So close she is that they can see her, run and touch her – then why any worry? If they see the slightest tension in Mummy's face, their happy faces start looking pitiable and helpless. Do nestlings being brought up in their nests go through similar experience when one of their parents is missing? But in the avian world, such tension must not be happening during their upbringing. This is the lot of human beings only.

She came out quietly to the veranda. She could feel the silently crawling night spreading within her being. She got down barefooted on the lawn and felt the pleasant chill of moist grass under her feet. Countless stars in the sky above, just as down below on earth countless persons scattered like spots, she one among them.

A dewdrop hanging from a leaf, about to fall … as if scared of falling; it will fall down on another leaf, but why on a leaf, why not on the grass or stony ground? In that case, it will cool that part of the ground.

From this dewdrop to the stars … vast universe; at this hour somewhere the darkness of night and somewhere the brightness of day … somewhere people in the midst of sleep, somewhere the hustle-bustle of people awake. How life comes suddenly into a foetus inside the womb … a tiny bit of air captured in the body … and it generates innumerable vibrations; when it leaves our body, we and our massive egos are reduced to a mere lump of earth. God, you are great … if this life given by you couldn't be sincere even to itself, how could it be to others?

The issue between Ramesh and her does not merely pertain to some misunderstanding or some lapse. Will she be able to love this man as she has been doing till now? Else, what's the difference between being his bed fellow and a prostitute? Ramesh and her own friends – Arvind, Shyam, Anant – who were proxy of things Ramesh lacked – they all created a balance which enabled her to give all her love and affection to her home, to caring for Ramesh and the children. Given her social limits and limitations, what could she give these friends of hers? Anant had said many a time that she was a giver through and through, just gave, but took nothing … but she alone knows what she was doing – like a butterfly she would fly here and there, extracting this from here and that from there and pouring it all on her *home*. If this balance goes awry, how can the home be saved?

Has she come to a decision … so quickly … but if every time the same voice emanates from within … then what…? Round the clock languishing in disgrace and hate. Even while living in the house, constantly feeling it's not hers anymore – had it been so, like before, if she observed anything askew in the house, wouldn't she have got up instantly to mend it? The compulsion of sleeping beside the man who had brutalized her and continue living in a city where there is no respect … today Shyam's wife comes to humiliate her, tomorrow Arvind's wife could come … while sitting in the office not a single moment passes unassailed by fears … if nothing else, Shyam or Arvind or Anant might come, and close on their heels, Ramesh … even the ringing of the phone scares her, compelling her not to lower her guard even for a moment …

How can one live like this? She moves back into the veranda.

This home. She has been here for the last seven years. Every single thing, big or small, in the house has been her handiwork … this swing in the veranda, the temple on the right, the bookcase in the drawing room housing her books collection, flower beds in front, kitchen garden in the backyard, and proper arrangement for watering the plants … in every nook and corner she can see her stamp. But how everything has become strange suddenly. The creeper bearing jasmine flowers on the pillar in the veranda kept on rising high and changed almost into a tree simultaneously with her transformation into a full luscious woman over the years. All this while, her daily routine was picking fresh white flowers and offering them at the temple. God! Now let this big flower too fall on your holy feet.

Dull sound behind … Ramesh is there. He brings two cane chairs and puts them down near Suvarna. They sit down. The night's silence broken intermittently by the watchman's warning cry. High above, twinkling stars stitched on the sheet of sky.

'I am sorry, darling,' Ramesh mumbles.

'Ramesh, now I've reached a point where these words have no meaning. Please feel free to bring out your revolver.'

'I lost control … I am terribly sorry.'

'No use harking back to what has happened. Had I left there and then, I could have prided myself on the decision having been entirely mine, but the tussle whether it was right or wrong would also have been there. Now I have to go. It won't be possible to live with you, Ramesh.'

'Such things happen, yaar! Haven't I asked for your forgiveness?'

'Even supposing what has happened is washed away by seeking pardon, and with the passage of time the incident has lost its sting, yet your thinking, the sole cause of it all, can't be wished away so easily. Even if it could be and I could be convinced that you don't think this way anymore, how can I run away from the fact that I don't love you anymore?'

'No big deal … but you stay. In our country, there are innumerable men and women who, all their lives, live as husband and wife. Do they continue to love ever so ardently? Come on, give up this silly thinking and don't trouble yourself unnecessarily.'

'I don't come in the category of the multitude, so I'm not obliged to practice all this sham. I won't be living with my parents either. I'm going to ask for a transfer.'

'Can't we settle this and come to an agreement? That you meet anybody you like barring these three persons with a solemn promise on my part that such an incident won't happen again.'

'I'm not prepared to accept that just because you are my husband, you will decide who I could meet and who I couldn't. It isn't just a matter concerning three or four persons, it's about that freedom which God has given me and which you want to usurp. But no need for argument. Even if you have no objection to my meeting these three persons, my decision will remain unchanged.'

'Why?'

'*Because I don't love you anymore*,' Suvarna was calm.

'May I ask who you do love then?'

'Not necessary that we stop loving one and at once start loving another … or loving the other has already begun and this has come to light only now. One can also live without loving anyone.'

'This is precisely what I am saying, All this lovey-dovey matter suits teenagers or your Anant-like friends … sick minds!'

'To ensure that the children don't get embroiled in it, if you agree, we can act normally so that they don't feel anything. Of course they will come to know eventually, but by that time they would have grown up mentally. I'll take them to my place and educate them there. You can visit them,' Suvarna revealed her mind.

'If I don't agree to this ....'

'Then tell me what you do want.'

'That you stay here.'

'That is just not possible. I'm not used to leading a humdrum existence. Moreover, I'm gradually learning to identify my beliefs and act on them.'

'It's possible that with the passage of time, your heartburn is washed away. After all, what I did was done in your interest and mine. Had I not stopped you now, when could I have done it? I tolerated it so far. Most likely, gradually you will appreciate this and may start feeling for me like before.'

'If that happens, I'll come back.'

'Which means you'll use me, no? You will go and come as it suits you.'

'No, I'll come back only if you are also ready for it. What I want for myself, I'll give you too. You are free and will remain so. Remember, even when I was with you, I didn't impose any restriction on you. I never objected to your relations with any man or woman. Suspicion, spying ... nothing of the sort.'

'These restrictions have not been imposed by me. They are dictated by the institution called marriage.'

'Marriage or, for that matter, any institution cannot be bigger than life, our lives. Somewhere these ties can be a compulsion, but in our case it needn't be so. My going away like this doesn't mean I'm leaving home. If you want to think so, it's up to you. If you want a divorce, I'll give it to you. My going away now will give me an opportunity to reflect dispassionately and calmly about my life and our conjugal relations. If I felt it was only a passing shadow that had embittered our relations and I still loved you, I would let you know. Living together thereafter will be with your consent. Right now I feel the need of living away from you.'

Ramesh got up in exasperation. 'I know – those ruffians wouldn't rest until they've destroyed my home. How twisted and warped your thinking is! Can't you walk straight? Oh God!'

Scarcely had he taken a few steps to go than he turned back. 'Okay, you may go. One day you'll realize your mistake. They all are your friends till you are beautiful … these goddamn debauches! And look here, you aren't going to take the children with you. They will be with me. Your ranting and raving like this will also make them sick. And please, end your antics early. Be done with what you want to do. Beside yourself, you are driving me crazy too.'

A man spluttering in rage and breaking down. Suvarna watched his show of anger before he went inside. He will go into the bedroom, drink water, make a beeline for the bed, and lie down. For some time he will stare at the ceiling, then will turn on his side and close his eyes. A little while later, the snoring will start.

Peace from top to bottom ... she hadn't had this feeling for quite some time ... maybe she experienced it hardly four or five times ... mostly in Anant's company.

Poor Ramesh! How will he live without her ... he is so dependent on her even for small things. Then should she stay and cheat on Ramesh as she hasn't done so far ... or cheat on him with his consent, go on cheating on him? Ramesh will be ready for this too. He's used to all those comforts and facilities that Suvarna makes available in the house, her presence that saves the house from having a deserted look, sustains the atmosphere and appearance of status, of a high-profile officer and a beautiful wife! Should she go on just trying to be a decoration piece in Ramesh's life and do nothing for herself?

Her house cloaked in darkness ... her house one of many similar houses in a row. Neon lights positioned at regular intervals along the street, emitting bright white light below. No sooner does the evening set in than the street hums with the buzzing of a multitude of impatient moths. Now, there is stony silence.

Suvarna had all along felt that she was on a voyage of self-discovery, but she was mistaken. What had gone on till now was actually aimless wandering – being influenced by just anyone, instant introduction ... the acquaintance transforming into intimacy. Just drifting, drifting, and reaching nowhere. No colour of your own. Red with 'A', blue with 'B'. For years she nursed the illusion of love for a man who gave her just one thing ... his name ... honorofic Mrs So and So.

In a flash, Suvarna had an urge to use her maiden name.

Not about Togetherness or Separation

The blazing sunshine sprawled across the sky, passing through the foliage of tall pine trees, descends on the ground in a mosaic of bright and dark spots, neither complete shadow nor complete sunshine. Afternoon gloom on the hills, the lone cry of a bird flitting across the tree. Thirst or restlessness …

Suvarna is walking under the trees … aimless, uncertain.

Couldn't instantly get the transfer, so she took leave and came away to be with her parents. After this break, she will find out about her new posting and go there directly … then new city, new job, new life …

As though the Suvarna of yesterday – whatever she was – has been left behind. That ceaseless running about every moment – from this situation to that, from one individual to another, from one assignment to another, often several situations, individuals, assignments simultaneously. Suvarna was under the delusion that it's only when she manages manifold things at the same time that she makes the best use of her energy and strength; it manifests the best of her personality. As though none else was equal to

Suvarna in that multitasking race and she had to run it alone. Since she left the race behind, she feels so light. As if, all that was superfluous peeled off automatically and has been sloughed away. There, all the time, she was with someone or the other … at times even to the point of tedium. Now her sole companion is herself.

It's a small town nestled in the hills, cooler, at a higher attitude, away from the razzle-dazzle of a popular hill station. Absorbed in its own beauty and serenity, located far from the hustle and bustle of city life, unsullied and clean, a tad sad. Below deep valleys chock-a-block with trees. Tall pines. Facing them, the undulating range of hills.

Her parents live here after retirement. She had no desire to apprise them about anything, but couldn't evade her mother's enquiring look. Now, of course, both of them are concealing it all from Papa. Mama says she will stay with Suvarna at her new posting. What sort of society is it that Suvarna can't live alone just because she is a woman?

She took to this way all of a sudden. Should she have given it some more thought? But if you get into the 'to-be-or-not-to-be' mode, you are unlikely to come out of it, you tend to drag. It can't be said that she reached a conclusion after due reflection. She vividly remembers – suddenly a ray of light burst showed the way ahead … and she hit the trail. Not that no nagging doubts arise in the mind … but there is more sadness, the pain of separating from those left behind.

She misses her younger son – so lean and thin despite her doting care. Whenever he saw her lying, he would come running, snuggle upto her, and bury his face in her tummy. He likes her bare fair midriff. He would rub his face on her midriff while Suvarna would be caressing his hair. Sometimes lying by her side, sometimes swinging on her neck, he would say, 'Mummy, you are so nice!'

What a coincidence that Anant also used to whisper the very same words, the only difference being 'Suvi' instead of 'Mummy'.

Guddu, my son! Your mummy is not at all nice. See, she came away leaving you behind, but I will come or my mama–papa both will come there and bring you to me. How can I stay away from my kids!

Where does this aromatic scent arise from? From the immovable hillocks, or from the twigs beyond sight, or the thick trunks of these trees sprawling across in multitudes – trunks, torn up from here and there due to dampness. These trees are not found on the plains .... Is it some characteristic of the soil or ground ... under plants and bushes, grass and weed, and debris scattered all over? The layer of dust on which Suvarna is walking, how can it be called ground? Then where is the ground ... below it ... where ... how far below...?

Until the other day everything was organized – up in the morning, getting ready in a jiffy, rushing to office, no end of work in the office, returning dog-tired, then household chores. Right from the morning tea up to the dinner, everything tied in the warp of 'time' and 'space'. The years to come were also clearly defined – the children would grow up, settle down in marital bliss, she and Ramesh would continue with their jobs. Friends – some common, some separate. Both would retire around the same time, growing old together. The whole plan was shattered to smithereens in one swift swoop. Everything seems to have fallen apart. Now what? And when she grows old?

Chug … chug … a non-stop monotonous sound emanating, as though from a train passing by a little afar. Or is it the wind passing through the trees or the leaves rustling? Below in the valleys, the afternoon wilderness is spread across. The tall hillock in front looking so dwarfish … let alone plants or hedges, not even a speck of grass is growing on the peak … bald.

Quite often, seated before her, Mama tries to read her thoughts. The sombre way she looks at her fills Suvarna with some kind of helplessness. There is something wrong with us Indian women. We are so much used to bondage that just a temporary break and we get impatient to return to the old set-up. Ah, my husband! Ah, my children! Oh hell! What husband – the man who sticks the label 'married' on your forehead and in lieu of a token dubious security shield arrogates to himself the right to torture you anyway anytime … And as for the children, they are only yours until they have matured. The moment they grow up, they become different persons – we want a colour TV, bring a video … our friends have in their houses, we aren't begging alms … and the day they see the faces of their wives, all the labour of love of the parents comes to nought … they brought us into the world, so had to bring us up … it was their duty, no obligation on us!

Unsavoury thoughts send a shiver down her spine … what's there that you can call yours. She tries to touch the afternoon breeze, gets a lukewarm feeling on the skin!

She has thrown herself here in the lap of nature. Earlier, she had lulled herself in the belief that every new contact added something to her. She might have succeeded to some extent … but one simple fact escaped her – if we are constantly with this person or that, then when are we with ourselves? If we keep soaking in impulses drawn from others, our own sensibility will go moribund in course of time. Unless we are in our own company, how will we identify ourselves and accomplish self-development? She thought she couldn't live without certain relationships, but now it looks that they weren't so vital after all. They did fill her life, but now that they aren't there, she doesn't feel all that empty either. Conversely, sometimes it appears they all were unnecessary burdens, and having cast them off she is feeling light. No accompanied baggage now, she can chill out and live freely.

Similarly, there was one thing more – the disease of radicalism! To go by reason alone. Whatever we are doing is right … very good. Employing sophistry, making exaggerated claims about insignificant acts; turning them into inflated balloons; strutting about safeguarding self-interest; floating about this or that official assignment, giving it wide publicity; we did this big work of the office and with such finesse and efficiency; nursing the illusion that we have all-round knowledge and versatile interests; we are highly educated and a thinking lot and our hobbies include literature, fine arts, performing arts; will open a dance school and share our art with others – in short, publicize one's talents and establish one's self-importance everywhere; restlessness to see yourself established as a connoisseur, a cognoscente in any intellectual field, a typical malice inflicting today's women!

Suvarna used to think that all these things and her several relationships would help her in her advancement, but in this obsession she was constantly sowing something or the other in each inch of her land – she forgot that if every inch of the land is infested with grass and weed, nothing else can grow there.

Suvarna closes her eyes ... now when there is nothing, everything is there ... the azure sky, bright sun, foliage, mountains, land ... wind caressing her face and touching every chord of hers, and every moment blowing along with her. Throw out everything from within, and then what will grow there will be real.

Let this God-given life flow in all humility ... no matter if our achievements remain nothing to boast of ... keep going under the trees ...

How far has she traversed?

Outside, someone is enquiring about Suvarna.

The voice has reached Suvarna, who is sitting inside. She has heard this voice so many times – at every turn, during her highs and lows, from near or far, soft or loud – that even if its faintest sound falls into her ears, she would recognize it, but instead of excitedly getting up and going out, she keeps sitting. On being informed about a visitor, Mama's eyes light up with hope – Ramesh has come to apologize, to take her back, her daughter will return, after all domestic quarrels are routine family affairs …

Mama comes out. Suvarna follows, her pace slow, and then she hears her own firm voice …

'Come, Anant, come in.'

Suvarna introduces the visitor to Mama as a friend from the city which she has left behind, but she can clearly detect from Mama's eyes that the real introduction that has reached her is that this is the man responsible for Suvarna's home being on the rocks.

Conversation revolving round the habitation, home, weather. In between tea, Mama scrutinizes Anant. Asks him probing questions. Her suspicion turns into certainty after coming to know that he is unmarried. Amidst all this, Suvarna is silent … just about participating in formal talk and soon returning to herself as if she has nothing to do with Mama or with Anant. Mama is rapidly firing questions at Anant to Suvarna's dismay. She can't look straight at Mama, sits with eyes downcast. But why … Suvarna tenses herself, sits up straight.

The tightness that had appeared on Mama's face immediately after her introduction to Anant is gradually fading out, but it is yet to be replaced by her trademark smiling countenance.

Anant is writhing within … Suvarna can see, maybe Mama too. Before either of the two ask to be left alone for some time, Mama gets up on her own.

Clouds are gathering over the habitation. Under cloud cover, the shapes of houses, street, bushes, and trees are getting darker. It looks like it will rain today, the season's first showers. A slight nip in the air.

Are they meeting for the first time? They wanted seclusion to converse, but now that they are alone, they are at a loss for words. Anant is just looking at Suvarna, his whole being melting. Like faint notes emanating from invisible sources … the silent sound of light rain dropping on leaves.

'You didn't even let me know,' the endearing complaint sounds like the twang of a tanpura.

'…'

'Learnt from your office that you'd applied for transfer, then taken leave. Didn't find you there, thought you must be here. Should I not have come?'

Huge raindrops descend on the hills. The scent of moist earth rises up and fills the atmosphere.

'What have you planned?' he shot the next question.

'Nothing!'

'You must have thought of something. Don't tell me that you simply came away?'

'There was perhaps no conscious thought. Thinking and yet more thinking led me nowhere. I acted on pure impulse.'

'Yes, sometimes I think this vast universe ... in it, this smallish earth and we people, mere dots, glued to it ... and we consider our big or small tomfoolery a laudable achievement. We nurse the illusion that whatever happens is done by us. At the most, we can do only what's apportioned to us, which is neither here nor there. Is it in your hands what Ramesh does? Was it ever so?

'Then when it appears that things are going against us, we go crazy – cursing ourselves, introspective, picking errors. It's nothing but sheer conceit on our parts to think that this action of ours will lead to such and such a reaction. Things happen despite ourselves. Our thinking makes very little difference, but puffed up as we are, we start thinking we're the masters of our destiny. That heady feeling subsides in no time when we're jolted by sudden shock – some mishap, someone's death, or an unpleasant experience as in your case and then belatedly we realize we're no better than non-entities, just figureheads, if at all. Entire mode of our thinking, attitude to life ... practically everything undergoes a sudden sea change. Oh, sorry! Here I go again, talking endlessly.'

'It feels good to listen to you.'

'But I have come to hear from you. What was the need for a transfer? Here suddenly...?'

'These are small things. What is important is which way the current is flowing, not the bubbles on the surface.'

'Then?'

'You yourself say there's no point in thinking too much,' a slight smile played on her lips.

'No, what I said was that there should be no pride about thinking. How can thinking stop till we're alive? In my opinion, you should return home. You won't be happy here.'

'Even you can be wrong for once. For your information, just before and after coming here, I continued to suffer from a strong guilt complex. Then I received a letter that opened my eyes. Ramesh had a regular affair with a woman ... they used to sleep together.'

'What? I can't believe....'

'I too wouldn't have, but this letter was from that very woman – Urvashi – she is from Ramesh's cadre. I know her ... she herself has confessed.'

'What can be her motive in writing to you?'

'Could be anything. What she's written is that she was very much pained to know what Ramesh had done to me.'

'Is she married?'

'No.'

'Then you can't rule out the possibility that Urvashi is planning to grab Ramesh by widening the rift between you two.'

'Quite possible. But this doesn't change the reality of that which existed between them. I did know that they were close friends, but never thought that it was to this extent. Despite this, Ramesh had the temerity to treat me the way he did.'

'You didn't think of going back at once on receiving the letter?'

'Any other woman in my place would have done that and busied herself in repossessing Ramesh. Had it been the earlier me, maybe I too would have done this. But now the very thought of this grabbing and gloating about it gives me a nauseous feeling. Thank God, I got this information. Now I'm spared the feeling of guilt that I'd left a faithful husband who didn't ever think of any other woman.'

'Can you say you're happy here?'

'If it were not a matter of being happy but of being less unhappy?'

'Suvarna! You seem to have grown up during this period and so quickly!' Anant's gaze began to sink into Suvarna's teary eyes like floating shells descending in a waterfall. Suvarna is dripping within herself like melted wax – rain inside! Getting up, she opens the window.

The rain has stopped. But with this brief shower, everything looks washed and wiped clean. Clouds of vaporous air, passing through hills, descending to fill the valley.

'I'm staying in Happy Home. If possible, come over in the evening … I want to have a long chat with you.'

'Anant, please don't ask me to meet you outside. Since I left home, it is as though I have lost the courage to meet anyone outside in private. Previously, I saw nothing wrong about it.'

'You find it wrong now?'

'No. Maybe yes … I want to have a total feel of the ground I'm now standing on.'

'Are you thinking of breaking up with Ramesh?'

'Don't know!'

'Children?'

'They are still there … might come here in a few days … let's see.'

'What do they want?'

'Poor kids, who cares for their choice. I'm missing them very much, Anant! How they must be living without me. Ramesh knows next to nothing about bringing up children. Nor has he any keenness for it. He's deliberately keeping them so that I may return and begin to live with him on his terms. I can't live without the kids. Poor darlings, no fault of theirs. Egos of two adults clash and it is always the children who have to suffer the most. This isn't fair.'

'That's why I advised you to return.'

Returning to the same place? The same despicable world … people wallowing in mud, such as Ramesh–Urvashi, Suvarna too on the same page, more or less. If somebody has a little purer feeling for another person, people like Ramesh will bring them down to the level of their narrow obscene thinking. People flinging their own mud on others!

'To live with Ramesh is somewhat like life imprisonment! Do you know since he dragged me like that, I haven't forgotten even for a moment that I've been living with a brute. Then it also occurs to me that what Ramesh has done to me, any other person in his place would have done the same.'

'Both of you should think about the children.'

'Ramesh knows my weakness. By keeping the children with himself, he's blackmailing me and will continue to do so. I don't like this doublethink of mine that I want independence and the children too. With all my education, I'm still an Indian woman. What'll happen to me, Anant?'

I had seen the play of myriad colours in those gorgeous eyes, but today I was witnessing such turmoil in them as I hadn't seen before. Turmoil … on being weighed down by, or rather crushed under such a heavy load of happenings of the past few days and the imponderables of the future that even shedding tears wouldn't bring her any relief, her mouth going dry instantly. Seeing her suffering from such close quarters, I too felt helpless. She was at that point of suffering where we are just alone.

'I'm filled with remorse whenever I think that I'm no less responsible for all this,' I said.

'No, you have given me a lot, or I would have gone on drifting. To be stable, to stand on your own … I have learnt that from you only. Else, I would have completely broken down long back.'

'I don't know what your final decision will be, nor do I know when we'll be meeting next, so I want to tell you right now … if at all I'm fortunate enough to spend my life with you, it'll be fulfilment of a dream, Suvarna….'

'I know fully well how deeply you love me. It's only that I don't consider myself worthy of you. There was something that moulded me like this … incomplete, a little askew, letting me remain stuck to fakes even at the cost of the genuine. Somewhere I bind myself gradually, but snap ties suddenly. Alas, if only I could sink completely in you as you are able to do in me! Till I'm able to do so, something will continue to prick my conscience. Often I suffer from an inferiority complex before you. Perhaps, there has been some serious shortcoming in my education and upbringing. Sometimes I feel I have been conditioned … a great deal has been soaked up.'

'You will not stop me if I wait for you, will you?'

'Don't know. In your company I've begun to understand a little, but at present I want one thing from you … these days don't be available to me. I don't want to be a weakling. Instead of weakening me, give me strength!'

'You know that….'

'Then don't come till I come out of all this, this way or that!'

She feels the glitter of tears in her eyes. Anant, smiling before her. Anant! It is only you who worry so much for me, understand me, bear with me. Your face didn't shrink a bit, brightened up on the contrary. I was seeking precisely this from you. It is not separation.

Anant has got up to go. He strolls leisurely towards her. She feels Anant's warm palm in her hair. She takes down his palm in her hands and kisses it. 'Don't be sad!'

Anant pats her hands….'Take care! Always remember that you are something for someone too, not just for yourself. That's why….'

Suvarna's eyelashes open and shut in quick succession, as if she collects some image inside her eyelashes, and then shuts them. Moist eyelashes, clasped hands like entangled flowers.

'Will give you a ring,' she says, as she used to do earlier.

Both laugh – first Anant, followed by Suvarna.

Emerging from the green valley, the whitish vapour of clouds is coming up, as if some welcome guest is returning. Then gradually, the increasing visibility of the desolate valley, now bathed and wiped clean by the clouds, sad but radiant.

22 June 1980

Suvarna has always brought out the best in me, inspired me to transcend shallowness and selfishness. For this very attribute, she had to pass through so many troubles. I'm one of the factors responsible for her predicament. My love. Love, which is the acme of humanity.

The sadness in me that had been under wraps, thanks only to Suvarna's company, is raising its head again, but now it appears to be my intimate friend. The journey with Suvarna has come to an end; unlikely that we will meet again. The pang of separation is there, but it doesn't look as if an integral part of mine has been snatched away from me. As though Suvarna is constantly with me, and will ever be.

Something luminous ceaselessly burns inside; the essence of our relationship perhaps – true bonding of souls. In this ruthless and near-insensitive world, this spirituality alone will give us strength to discharge our responsibilities. With its help, bearing our share of grief, we'll be able to stand our ground. Soul-bonding … what a wide dimension it adds to life! Had Suvarna not come into my life, it's doubtful if at all this vastness would have opened before me.

My heart isn't in this city any more … to live in the midst of a culture where, in the guise of love, something else is being touted! Love should rub out our ego, strengthen our moral fibre, sincerity, and selflessness. In contrast, here there's motivated love … cold and calculating – when, how, who for, how far; it ought to get me something, take away nothing, never ever torment me – this cautious approach to love, always safeguarding oneself … only makes us cunning and crafty. I won't live here anymore. My needs are sparse, so no hitch in leaving the city. Will live in a village. Home…? If, in the concept of home, sensitivity to others' problems and hardships is most significant, then the very sharing of the joys and sorrows of every village family will constitute my home. For occupation and little income to meet bare necessities, freelance journalism can be taken up. Will draw attention of villagers to their pressing problems and seek solutions. I can also take to farming in partnership with somebody. If the desire to amass riches is not there, just anything can be done to manage a couple of square meals.

Reason scoffs at me that this is sheer idealism, a pipe dream, as craftiness has permeated down to villages too. Even then, in the small entity of a village, I will attempt to stem the onslaught of this craftiness. I might not succeed, but a small beginning will certainly be made.

I can vividly see what l ought to do. The love that surges for one person, why not disperse it among all? Graciousness, compassion, empathy for humanity at large. Service in place of love. How amazing that the fountainhead of all these noble sentiments is love itself!

I tantalizingly look at all these ideals … will I ever be able to rise up to their lofty heights? Suvi, I badly need your company. Your going away … it seems the passage of life is nothing but a sequence of one good thing after another leaving us. How hard it is to be away from you, so tormenting; yet this torment is also a beacon, a beacon whose light will guide me.

Suvarna and Anant, sitting cuddled up against each other, watching a marriage ceremony. It's some village … a cluster of mud houses forming a small circle. In the middle of an open courtyard, the bride and bridegroom doing the ritual rounds of the tulsi plant housed in the courtyard. The girl is wearing a sari dyed in turmeric water. A thick coating of kohl has been applied to the boy's eyes, a kohl mark adorns his forehead. This is making Suvarna laugh; she's cosying up to Anant.

'That black spot on the forehead is to protect him from the evil eye,' Anant is telling her.

Mud houses covered with dust. In the middle, a dusty path for bullock carts, dust assailing the nostrils causing laboured breathing. Suvarna's feet get stuck in the dust time and again. To free her feet, she stretches her hands around to find support. There is nothing, no one, only air … Suvarna is getting alarmed.

Now that path has shrunk into a short, narrow pedestrian track passing through an avenue of trees. The dust gone … there are clouds touching Suvarna before floating away. The moisture gives her a shiver. She is walking with Anant, hand in hand. They have climbed up. When they look down, they see Ramesh's jeep standing in the middle of the dusty path. Ramesh is in uniform … he is making enquiries about Shyam Mohan from the villagers … Shyam has absconded, he's become a dacoit. Which house is he hiding in?

Suvarna and Anant watch Ramesh's anger from above, and then exchange glances. Their faces are blank … simply looking at each other. Anant asks, 'Where did you come from at 2 am, in the dead of the night?' Suvarna says, 'From Arvind's.' Anant takes her face in his hands and says, 'Your eyes are so sad, your face is looking so lean.' Anant is looking at her with love; he picks her up in his arms. Suvarna has turned into a child, clad in a frock, cradled in Anant's lap.

'Suvarna is here with me,' Anant calls Ramesh, pointing to Suvarna in his lap.

Ramesh has seen them. Quickly climbing up, he reaches up to them. Suvarna is standing close to Anant, so close as if almost glued to him. Ramesh is happy to find Suvarna. Holding Suvarna's hand, he walks away without even looking at Anant. They are descending and going towards the jeep. While walking, Suvarna cranes her neck again and again to see Anant.

Dust … bullock carts are passing … it's a marriage procession, returning with the bride. A pall of dust rises and covers them. Nothing is visible.

'Ramesh, where's Anant gone? Look for him….'

'Only a little while ago, he was here. Are we to take him along with us?' Ramesh asks.

'Yes.'

Ramesh looks at Suvarna and then begins to laugh. Both enter into the cloud of dust in search of Anant. They are separating leafy branches to find him.

One very old tree, thick roots even on the surface and spread wide. They see something reddish near a root. Suvarna runs towards it. It's a big earthen lamp … Suvarna picks it – we'll keep it in the home temple … during Diwali, we'll light it first, then light the other lamps with its flame….' she's saying.

Waves of happiness in the dream, Suvarna is turning over in her sleep … jerks. She gets up. Draws back the curtain from the window … morning brightness sprawled across the sky … golden clouds!

Rain on the hills …

Sweeping the hills with a long and strong current, filling the valleys, rustling and whizzing through leaves, this menacing wind … as if its violently spiralling current will blow away a whole habitation.

A shudder running through the hills … uncanny sounds echoing all around … everything looks like it's flying helter-skelter, goodness knows, in what direction! Rain comes riding on a menacing thunderstorm.

Nature in its fury seems bent upon wrenching away from its secure hideout this decked-up and cosily entrenched world of ours and annihilating it.

When it stops raining, an irritating humidity prevails all round, damp and clammy; below and above. Sunshine far-far away.

Suvarna keeps looking, sometimes from the outside, sometimes from the inside. As if it is not an ocean of air, as if it's an infinite expanse of time, emphatically declaring its august presence with gigantic whacks and smacks.

Saying anything sounds like prattling. When she hears people talking, every word strikes her like a hammer blow. Don't say anything, just be a mute spectator. Apart from the daily grind of getting up, finish the morning ablutions, bathing, and the rest, she has nothing left to do except to keep sitting and gazing into space … heart and mind in a languid mode. If only we could get fully absorbed in what is before us. To completely sink into something – individual, object, or idea – why this can't be construed as togetherness, marriage, or love? The rest of the life is nothing but separation, passing in quest of such togetherness. Short stint relationships instead of a single lengthy one, a little reserve built into them of course. They can be with anyone, with even a husband. Instead of being completely absorbed, every time in a different situation, getting into and coming out of involvements. Short-duration marriages! Ramesh.

Or anyone else. Whatever she could get from them was Suvarna's! The rest wasn't hers, so it went away. Why grieve over something that didn't belong to her? Instead of getting stuck in the past, keep moving, engaged or disengaged in new things, new people …

But wasn't this what she was doing earlier? If one could only emulate water when it lands on a lotus leaf – on the leaf, yet detached from it! Could she remain as detached as that? Just one hiccup – breaking away from Ramesh. And she's got herself so severely bruised.

'Didn't wash your hair today also?' Mama asks. She's always on the lookout to trap her, so that she may give Suvarna a push. Like shunting of train bogies, where one bogie gives a push to another bogie to get it moving. Suvarna doesn't want to remember anything from the past, but Mama, in passing, will say something or the other to push her there. If nothing else, she will bring up Ramesh's name on some pretext or the other.

To live in that kind of captivity for the sake of a person like Ramesh? She would have continued to do so, had those unpleasant incidents not torn the mask off Ramesh … and then her whole life would have gone waste. But if on some particular occasion, someone's lava-like anger spews out, can it be deemed to be his real nature? How can she form an opinion about Ramesh on the basis of a stray skirmish or two?

'How long will it go on like this?' Mama has suddenly decided to confront, to take the bull by its horns.

'What, what will go on?' Mama's blunt question has raised Suvarna's hackles. Life is too short to warrant such questions.

'Your moving about with unwashed hair. Why take it out on your hair? Not shampooing it isn't going to solve the problem.'

'Will do it. Didn't feel like, so didn't … not because of….'

'Or so you claim,' Mama has got her in her grip and sits down firmly. 'Must fight it out, my child!'

Mama is still stuck in the same groove, with those very words that Suvarna used to hear right from childhood. She doesn't know that in the meantime, Suvarna has met and interacted with someone who is not so aggressive, nor does he think it necessary to be so … in fact the very opposite, mellow, soft, gentle.

The window pane is hazy with a layer of frost. The big pine tree outside appears dotted with black spots. Suvarna takes a piece of cloth, wipes the glass pane, and opens the window. A strong gust of wind, after blowing through the drenched leaves of the tree, passes by and sprays a few drops on her face. Suvarna's eyes close in bliss.

Gentle puffs of air, few and far between, taking her into the infinite … tiny droplets stretching out into cool vastness. Where's she reaching … the blue of the sky so bright and clear … radiance all round. Feeling very light, she is on a flight, cascades of joy sprouting from every fibre of her being and forming a wide current, flowing, floating unhindered. The very embodiment of sweetness, she longs to get lost in *Anant*, in the infinite.

Anant! Look! I have reached there! Though I had to crawl, had to struggle, at last I've reached there, the peak you managed to scale. Yes … something is stirring up within. I can feel it … now … the very same sensation I used to see you immersed in.

You were right, Anant. That living like a libertine, always shrewd and watchful … calibrated and calculated choice for future course of life … acting all the time in an arbitrary way … all this is nothing before getting drenched like this. What a paradox! Bondage unbinding you!

Seeing the window pane still dirty, Suvarna throws away the piece of cloth and begins to wipe the glass pane with a corner of her sari.

'Mama, you said you liked Anant.' I wish to be with you, Anant. If I cannot be with you, let me at least talk about you!

'Yes, I liked him very much.'

Mama's face has softened, Suvarna can visualize even without turning round. Mama has been mumbling Anant's name for the last couple of days. When she saw that Suvarna doesn't react when Ramesh's name is mentioned, she seems to have inferred that Suvarna is not going back to him. But how has she reached this conclusion? Or, maybe, she's begun to take Anant's name so that Suvarna doesn't continue to languish, brooding all the time, but comes to some decision. Suvarna turns round. Mama's eyes indicate her desire that Suvarna sit with her, no matter, even for a short period.

'You met him so briefly, yet you've begun to like him?' Suvarna asks with a pleasant surprise.

'If there's no room for doubt, won't things seem as clear as they are?'

'What do you like about him?' Suvarna sort of lost in thought, someone should speak, say something about you, Anant!

'This will need some thinking … and then perhaps heaps of positive things will come to light. It's evident he talks straight from the shoulder. Such a person won't lie, must be very sincere ….'

Suvarna comes and sits beside Mama. The glass pane is completely clear now! The window has been shut, even then the tree outside is fully visible, wiped clean – beautiful.

'Do you love him?'

Suvarna is startled at Mama's question and the sweetness of her tongue. She understands that instead of exploring slowly, advancing like sunshine, Mama has made a sudden sally … lest Suvarna get up, leaving the matter hanging. She wants a firm and quick decision from Suvarna.

Mama pauses on her silence. Suvarna gazes long at Mama in happiness for what she's just spoken. The very thought that Mama likes Anant fills brightness in her.

'Suvarna, there's no sense in your living like this. And why at all should you? What do you lack – you're educated, even now beautiful, get a decent salary. I'll have no objection, dear. I will make your papa understand.'

'Mama, the problem with you is that you love me so much and are so simple. You've understood so quickly that Anant and I like each other. But can you believe it when I say that Anant does not want me to leave my home or Ramesh.'

'Really! Is he a coward … or hesitant because of the children?'

'Neither. He said he would wait for me.'

'Oh, how nice! I told you, he's a very good boy!'

Mama's words got embedded within Suvarna, as though they were always hers, never from outside. No sooner is the sluice gate of the dam opened than a massive stream of water gushes down … Anant, I'm coming, here I come …

The onrushing stream pouring down into the dam-bucket flows onward, but quickly turns back … now split into waves, forward and backward waves clashing, waves flowing helter-skelter, going into a spin due to self-inflicted lashes … what commotion and chaos … whirlpools are formed, eddies below looking like climbing on the downward rush of water. The impatience of the stream to return to the source!

Anant, I want to come to you … but why don't I find the courage to break and abandon everything behind … where will I find it? As if somebody holds me back … why don't I run up to you … why am I afraid that you may also turn up to be another Ramesh? Then what...? I don't want to lose you!

My home … children … I don't want to leave them, Anant. But then, why have I come away leaving them behind? I want to go back, but why don't I … why am I inching towards you only?

The jumbled chain of conflicting thoughts make Suvarna squirm on the sofa.

'Darling!' Mama's face has gone taut.

'Mama, how strong Indian women happen to be! They can live with any type of husband; even when they have no love for him, they can pass their whole lives with him; they can reform dissolute husbands; abandoning their husbands, they can go with their lovers and can also distance themselves from husbands, though worshipping them in their hearts. A woman confined so far within the four walls of her house suddenly stirs out, takes up a job, and brings up children under her own steam. Mama, I can live alone.'

'Easier said than done. Even if you somehow manage to live alone, will people let you live singly? This male-oriented society and a beautiful woman! Vulnerable like a lamb or deer astray in a forest. Presently, you will be in the company of someone or the other, but one day you won't be as beautiful … then no one would be there. Right now you can't even imagine the utter loneliness, which will then overtake you.'

'If someone happens to be with me even then?'

'There is no one like that.'

'No Mama, there is one … Anant … He is different….'

An image parades before Suvarna's eyes.

Anant and herself ... both old ... walking hand in hand, sometimes enjoying the sight of garden flowers, sometimes sharing thoughts about the life of a boy on the roadside.

Her eyes have become moist. There was a time when it was near impossible for her to cry ... now tears make an appearance at every little excuse. Still she's prone to hiding her tears, even from Mama. Then something begins to writhe within, about to come out, anytime.

Alarmed, she gets up suddenly. Opening the window, she leans on it and cranes her neck outside. Her eyes misty with tears ... Ramesh, you didn't treat me with dignity due to a human being ... why did you behave in such an appalling way ... what right did you have to go to such an extent...?

The deep valley laden with dense trees ... silent ... desolate. A sound is spiralling up and down. A heart-rending scream ... the wailing of a bird ... crashing against trees ... rising and falling, going deep down into the valley, rising again towards the sky ...